I0451373

Capsized

Murrells Inlet Miracles, Volume 4

Laurie Larsen

Published by Laurie Larsen, 2019.

CAPSIZED

First edition. January 22, 2019.

Copyright © 2019 Laurie Larsen.

ISBN: 978-1386174288

Written by Laurie Larsen.

I dedicate this book to the talented extreme athletes who so generously shared their time and expertise with me. Any mistakes that remain involving competitive yacht sailing or marathon running are certainly not their fault. They're all mine! Thank you to you all, and I hope you love the book:

Charity Monroe

Tim McKenney

Paul McNamee

Tricia Martin

Capsized
Book 4: Murrells Inlet Miracles
Laurie Larsen

God "overseas" everything....

For nursing student Sadie Flynn, life is about helping those in need and decompressing with the thrill of extreme sports. After witnessing the destruction of her parents' marriage, Sadie wants nothing to do with love and romance. She's fine setting goals and achieving them alone—without a man to derail her plans.

Personal trainer and competitive yacht sailor, Jett Martin is a disappointment to his father, who always wanted his son to follow in his footsteps, as a tough military fighter. But Jett is nothing like his father. With his new invention gaining interest in the sailing world and an upcoming competition to prove his worth, Jett is on his way to his own version of the top. But when an injury threatens to destroy his chances for credibility and a lucrative future, he knows he needs help.

The courageous and risk-taking Sadie is the answer to his prayers. With his expertise and her strength, they're an unbeatable pair. With physical attraction tempting them, Sadie and Jett must keep their eyes on the prize. But God has other plans. As they face adversity and danger, will God's will have them racing toward one another instead of the glory of the win?

Chapter One

Sadie Flynn breezed into the kitchen, her mind fixed on her To Do list for this sunny May day. No time to enjoy the beach or the sun, much to her dismay. She pulled open the cabinet, extracted her travel coffee mug, and turned to the coffee pot. Half a pot of the elixir sat there already. She glanced around the room. Her dad sat at the kitchen table, enjoying a cup.

"Earth to Sadie," he said, then chuckled.

"Sorry. Did you say something to me?"

"Just 'good morning.' Your mind is obviously somewhere else. What's going on in there?"

She grinned and rolled her eyes. Being focused had served her well in her lifetime, in general, but sometimes it made her come off as ditzy. Or uncaring. And those traits were the furthest from the truth.

"Busy day today, Dad. I've got to swing by the college and enroll in my summer semester classes."

He stood and carried his empty plate to the sink. "One step closer to becoming a Registered Nurse." He leaned in and placed a kiss on her cheek. "I'm proud of you."

She took a moment to soak in his affection. She and her dad: a team, a twosome. The Dynamic Duo. It had been only her and him for so long, she could barely remember a time when there were three. Before her mom's health deteriorated, it was her dad who took care of her. Her mom had never shown interest in being a full-time mom, so it was lucky for Sadie that her dad filled in the gaps. But after her mother's car accident, and the resulting head injury that caused her to get worse and worse for years, Sophie and her dad had become a tight, well-functioning team.

Burying her mother last summer was not as sad as it probably should have been. Her death was totally expected and represented the final chapter in a tragic life.

Dad pulled away from his daughter with a friendly wink. "What else?"

Sadie cleared her head of sad memories. "Then, to the gym. I've only got a week left before the marathon, so I've got some training to do."

"Good for you. Break a leg."

"That may be appropriate for an actor, but I believe it's a jinx for an athlete."

Shaw chuckled. "Okay, then how about, don't break a leg?"

"Better. And what about you? What are you up to today?"

"Annual shots for the Anderson cattle herd, and then heading over to the Myrtle Beach Zoo to care for a few animals that are under the weather."

Sadie smiled. Her dad didn't have a job like most fathers did. He never sat in a desk chair behind a computer, didn't even have an office. As a large breed veterinarian, his patients were out in the fields and barns all around the Grand Strand, South Carolina. He spent most of his time in his truck driving to where the animals were and caring for them. He loved treating all animals, but especially the big ones, wild or domestic.

"And are you seeing your lady love today?" Sadie turned her head and noticed the flush of pink that traveled up her dad's neck. After a long stretch of no love or affection in his life, he had met the right woman. Some things were worth waiting for. Shaw and Nora were distinct opposites, but proof of the old adage that opposites attract.

"Sure."

So that was all the answer she was going to get about her dad's love life. She laughed, not expecting any different.

"Well, have a great day. See you tonight." They both wrapped up their breakfasts and headed out.

Later in the day, Sadie drove to Fitness Giants, the gym she'd been attending for several years. Workouts were a huge part of her life, especially since she'd started running marathons. Recently, she'd set a goal for herself: run a marathon in each of the fifty states. At age twenty-two, she'd already run five. Next week's race, in North Carolina, would bring her to a half dozen.

She dropped off her bag in the locker room, then found her way to the weight room. This week, her training plan called for light cross training with weights and elliptical, as well as some short runs, making sure her body kept active, but not overworked. She picked up free weights and started her lifting.

"Hey Sadie," came a voice behind her. She turned.

"Oh, hi, Jett."

"Training for something in particular?" Jett Martin was the personal trainer she'd worked with two years ago when she decided to start her marathon career. He'd given her a custom work out program to prepare her body and mind, and she'd followed it for every race since.

"Yep. I'm running a marathon in North Carolina next weekend."

"Awesome. You ready?"

"Should be. Still following the Jett Martin fitness plan," she said with a smile as she returned the ten-pound weights and grabbed the twelve.

"Well, then you can't lose." He turned away while he studied the form of his client, then turned back quickly. "If we both have time, how about a smoothie later and a chat to catch up?"

"Sure." Sadie smiled to herself, pleased that he'd suggested a catch-up. He'd been instrumental in getting her trained and in shape for running and she'd enjoyed working with him. He was tough and demanding when he needed to be, but also encouraged her and taught her how to take it easy on her body when necessary. As a trainer, he was the perfect combination of hard and soft. In the almost two years since she stopped working with him, she'd excelled as a marathoner. But it would be fun to find out what was new with him.

She pulled her eyes away from him when a faint heat settled on her neck. In addition to his talents, he was easy to look at. Tall, tanned, longish chestnut hair, a body as tight and fit as you would expect from a personal trainer. He was a handsome guy, no doubt about it. His biceps bulged as he helped his client, a tiny young woman probably no more than a hundred pounds, lift the weights back to the frame. "Good job," he was saying to her with a broad smile. Encouraging her, helping her achieve her goals.

Sadie put down her weights and walked purposely away from Jett, heading for the elliptical machine. And away from the odd attraction she'd just experienced. Time to get in some light cardio. As she started moving her legs, she glanced back at him for a moment. He was certainly a worthy person to be attracted to. However, she had already decided ... love was not for her. At least not at this point in her life. She had too many goals to accomplish to worry about a man. She was solid: a strong, single woman, working toward her own life and fitness goals. She was right on track. Why would she weaken her resolve and allow a man to worm his way into her heart? She refused to be derailed.

After all, she'd seen what happened to her mother and father when they fell in love. It led to nothing but heartache. Why would she ever allow that to happen to her?

She focused on the work she was doing on the elliptical. She would have a smoothie with Jett, she would chat and fill him in, but she would consider him only as a fitness partner. Nothing more.

~ * ~

Jett Martin held a palm up in the air, offering it to his new client, Tiffany. "High five."

She slapped it and grinned. She had worked hard today and had every right to be pleased with herself. But one strong workout didn't mean she was done. "Good job today, Tiffany. I want you to go soak in the hot tub for at least twenty minutes and take it easy the rest of the day. Tomorrow your workout plan calls for a two-mile jog."

She rolled her eyes. "I'd rather work out in the gym than run any day."

"You can do a run/walk combo if two straight miles proves challenging. Fitness is all about working up to the goal, not getting there immediately."

She patted his shoulder. "Yes, Coach. See you Friday for more torture." She chuckled and went off to the shower.

He cleaned up the station, then headed to the front desk. Time for a break, and he hoped Sadie had stuck around. A few years ago, she'd had the spirit of an athlete and the dedication of a workhorse. She was a machine, and that mindset was required for someone who wanted to perform at the highest levels. He looked forward to hearing about her marathon experiences.

He walked to the smoothie bar and was pleased to see that she sat there, waiting for him, a pink concoction in a cup sitting in front of her. He waved, then pointed to the bar. She nodded. Jett stood in a short line and waited, then ordered a strawberry smoothie with protein added. He took it and joined Sadie at the table. "Great to see you. You look like you're doing well. Strong and fit."

Sadie laughed. "Yep, you got me started and now I can't quit."

"Guilty."

"But I love it. I seriously do. I love pushing my body to its limits, and I'm continually amazed at what it can do."

"And getting that adrenaline rush."

Sadie nodded enthusiastically. "There's nothing like it."

Jett swallowed a mouthful of his drink. "So, marathons. Your event of choice?"

"Yeah, I guess so. I've done five of them now, and my sixth one is next weekend. I've set a goal to run one in every state of the U.S."

"Nice," he said with admiration.

She looked at the table. "I've always finished, but now I'm working on breaking my personal best time at each and every race. I want to start finishing in the medals of my age bracket."

He blew a breath out. "Tough to do because you're so young. Lots of strong competition there."

She gave him a fond smile. "Yeah but it's worth working for. If a woman my age is at the top, it might as well be me."

He nodded, a surge of pride flowing through him.

"So, what are you working toward?" she asked. "Do you have an event coming up?"

Jett looked into her eyes and noticed, not for the first time, that her eyes were a gorgeous and unusual golden color. They attracted attention due to their uniqueness, and he strove to get his mind back on her question. "Did I ever tell you what my sport was, when I was working with you? My passion, shall we say?"

She frowned. "Not that I remember."

"Sailing. I grew up on boats. My dad spent some years as a world-class sailor and I always wanted to follow in his footsteps. I had my own Sunfish from the time I was ten and when I was sixteen I graduated to a Laser."

"What's a Laser?" she asked.

"It's a more complicated boat, an eleven-foot sailing dinghy. It's a faster class of racing dinghies."

"Isn't a dinghy like a lifeboat?"

He chuckled. "Yes, in fact, they do refer to lifeboats and inflatable rafts as dinghies. But I'm talking about a big sailing vessel built for speed."

"Wow, so you compete in races?"

"Yep. I love it." He finished his drink and circled in his chair to face the trash can. He made a basketball toss and sunk it.

"How far do you race?"

"For dinghy races, we race around the buoys. In most cases, they use an Olympic Triangle course, which is six legs, the first three being a triangle and the last three to windward, leeward, and finishing to windward. The entire race can take anywhere from twenty minutes to a hundred minutes."

Sadie lifted her smoothie and tapped it on the tabletop, then took another sip. "That's really cool. You are a true ocean kid, aren't you? Sailing boats on the ocean is truly in your blood. And so is that crazy nautical vocabulary. I swear I don't know what half those words mean. Are you sure you're speaking English?"

"Yeah." He grinned at her. "But now I've moved on to sailing yachts."

"Holy mackerel!"

"My dad was racing long distance while I was doing the shorter courses. I crewed for him on a few ocean transits. When he upgraded to a newer vessel, he handed his yacht down to me." He pulled his phone out of his shorts pocket, tapped into it and showed her his photo gallery. "Here it is. The Majestic."

She leaned closer to see the photos. "That's the name of it?"

"Yep."

"I see why. Wow. This thing is huge and beautiful. Do you have a crew?"

"No. I sail it single-handed." He looked down and swiped through several pictures. "The Majestic's thirty-three feet long with sails fifty feet in the air. She's a big girl to handle on my own, but that's why I love her. She's a challenge."

Sadie laughed out loud. "That put an interesting image in my mind. Thank you for that."

Jett chuckled along with her.

"What kind of racing do you do with the Majestic?"

"Longer distance, not on a course, but in the open seas. It's a huge rush. I'm preparing for a long-distance race right now in fact. Whenever I'm not here, I'm out on the yacht trying to get my nautical miles in."

Sadie leaned back in her stool, shaking her head. "I could learn a lot from you. Not just about running, either. I've got some interest in extreme sports, and long-distance yacht sailing sounds pretty extreme."

"What kinds of extreme sports are you looking at?"

"I don't know. Something to get the blood pumping. Like, rock climbing, skydiving. I've never done any of it, but I want to."

Jett's gaze rested on her face and a flicker of attraction awakened inside him. This was the type of woman he should be interested in. She could keep up with him from an adrenaline-seeking standpoint. She was a daredevil like he was. She probably couldn't care less about girly stuff: doing her hair and makeup, wearing high fashion clothes. She always looked great but didn't appear to put much effort into her looks. Why did he always seek out girls that were the direct opposite of Sadie? Why was he drawn to petite, showy females: arm candy to accompany him places but not partake in his interests with him? Maybe if he started dating a girl like Sadie, his relationships would last longer than a few months, which was his record so far.

Sadie frowned and looked confused. "What is it, Jett?"

He jerked his gaze away. He must've been staring for too long. "Oh, nothing, I was just wondering if you'd want to go out to the marina with me and see the Majestic in person?"

Sadie gasped. "Seriously? I'd love to. Is there room for me on there? Can you take me for a ride?"

"Sure. Can you swim?"

Sadie smirked. "Can I swim? I grew up in Murrells Inlet. Of course, I can swim!"

"Okay, okay," he said, palms out, delighted by her feistiness. "I'll be heading over there this afternoon, about four. Are you free?"

She thought for a moment and then nodded. "Yeah, I'll do it. I want to check this thing out."

An unexpected shot of happiness soared through his body. "Meet you here at four. I'll drive you over."

Chapter Two

After a busy day of registering for classes, physical training and buying textbooks, Sadie met Jett at the gym at four o'clock sharp. She spotted him leaning against his pick-up truck, waiting for her. He shifted his weight and approached her with a smile.

"Ready?" he asked.

"Can't wait."

They got into his truck and soon they were taking the very familiar route to the famous MarshWalk in Murrells Inlet. The town carried the moniker of Seafood Capital of South Carolina, and the MarshWalk was a large reason why. A half mile of wooden boardwalk featuring one seafood restaurant after another, all offering beautiful views of a natural saltwater estuary that channeled to the Atlantic Ocean. On summer evenings, artisans of all types ... painters, sculptors, leather workers, jewelry makers ... occupied booths along the boardwalk, selling their wares to tourists and locals alike. Sadie couldn't count the number of times she'd been here in her life. Probably in the thousands.

"You dock your sailboat at the MarshWalk?" she asked.

"Yes, right now I am. At the far south end, where the Crazy Sisters Marina sits. They offer dockage for boats."

"Cool."

He pulled into the lot and she followed him to the boat. Or, was boat the wrong word? It seemed to minimize this magnificent sailing vessel. It was so much more than a boat. "Oh Jett," she exclaimed breathlessly. "This is beautiful!"

His dimples made an appearance along with a pleased smile. "Thanks. Like I think I told you, she belonged to my dad. He gave her to me about four years ago. Now, she's all mine."

"My goodness." Sadie walked the length of the yacht on the dock. "How long did you say?"

"Thirty-three feet."

"And you operate this thing all by yourself?"

"Yep. I mean, when I take friends out I give them a job. But when I'm competing, it's all me, baby."

"Amazing." Sadie reached out and drew her fingers over the red, white and blue painted name—The Majestic—along its white surface. She tilted her head back and took in the long pole that stretched far into the sky.

"That's the mast," Jett explained. "You just wait till we get the main sail up on it. It's a thing of beauty."

She wiped her hands on her shorts. This would be an education that she was really looking forward to. "Tell me what to do."

Jett laughed. "Here," he said, holding out a hand. "Come aboard. Watch your feet."

She placed her hand in his, trying to ignore the shot of electricity that passed between their joined palms. She stepped down into the boat and once he'd made sure she found her footing, he moved to the lines that tied the vessel to the dock. Within moments, he'd untied the boat and jumped in. Inside the yacht, he hurried into action, moving swiftly around the deck, from stem to stern, checking whatever it was a boat captain checked, and then positioned himself behind the steering wheel in the back.

"Ready to hit the high seas?"

"Sure am."

He turned over the engine and expertly maneuvered the ship backward out of its tight slip, turned the wheel quickly to reposition it, then motored out of the marina and into the open channel of water. Within fifteen minutes, he had steered the boat to the spot where, Sadie knew, the inlet met the ocean. The waves were bigger, and the color of the water took on a deeper, darker tone.

"Here we go." Jett moved to the center of the cabin. Near the long expanse of the mast, he climbed up on a higher level and checked the sails, currently furled and secured. He removed the securing lines and manually tugged on the folds of the sail, preparing it to rise. Once he was satisfied, he used a metal contraption and quickly rotated the handle, faster and faster.

First Sadie focused on his tanned biceps peeking out from his t-shirt sleeve, but soon her attention was dragged away from that pleasant view, to the results of his work. The appearance of a massive sail traveling up the mast, as high as it could go.

"Okay, that's the mainsail. Now I've got to do the jib."

"What's that?"

"The secondary sail, about half the size of the main."

She tucked that knowledge away in her mind and watched while he moved gracefully to another section of the boat and rotated the handle again. Soon both sails were up, flapping in the wind. Back behind the steering wheel again, he turned the helm and cut the engine. The yacht leaped forward in the water, powered only by the wind. Soon they were sailing, chopping up distance in the big expanse of open seawater.

"This is amazing!" she exclaimed.

He made his way over to her, stood behind her and rested his hands on her shoulders. "Sure is. Never gets old."

They sailed, and Sadie filled her senses to overflowing. The sun warmed her skin and the water made a calming lapping sound. Seabirds flew overhead, cawing and announcing their pleasure with the beautiful day. She gazed up at the cloudless blue of the sky pairing with the blue of the water on the horizon. Soon she could no longer see land in any direction, and it was easy to convince herself that she and Jett were the only humans on this vast stretch of ocean. In that moment, she was immensely thankful to have spent her growing-up years on this coast, raised amidst the sand, the sun, and the saltwater in this, one of the most scenic places God had ever made. She closed her eyes and sent a silent prayer, in recognition.

She leaned over the side of the cockpit, watching the streamlined hull cut through the water. Stretching her arm over the side, she reached down, but they sat too high to reach the water. She straightened and made her way cautiously to the bow and imagined the scene in Titanic, where Leonardo and Kate lean out over the stern, arms thrown out, wind blowing in their faces. Then she moved to the base of the massive sails and gazed up, up, up, observing the late-afternoon sun shining through the sailcloth.

She whirled around to face Jett, a blissful smile on her face. He grinned back. No words were necessary. They were in sync. This adventure was something they both treasured.

They sailed, the wind powering their journey for about twenty minutes. Then Jett said, "Want to take the helm?"

She jumped forward, caught herself from losing her balance and grabbed hold of the side of the boat. "The what?"

"The steering wheel is the helm. Want to steer?"

"Of course." More slowly this time, she carefully put one foot in front of the other while the ship made its way through the waves. Holding on to whatever she could find, she finished her journey to the helm and scooted in behind it, standing next to Jett.

He gazed up at the sails. "Actually, maybe not. The wind has really picked up."

Sadie shrugged. "That's okay."

Jett grinned at her. "Love the spirit, but the most intimidating thing for a new sailor is to take the helm, particularly on a windy day."

Sadie looked upwards. The thrill of slicing through the water in a big magnificent yacht made her heart race. How much more exciting would it be to steer it herself? "You'll be here to help me, right?"

Jett chuckled. "Yep." He moved to the side, offering her the helm. "Go ahead and take hold."

She did, and everything seemed to be fine. She couldn't tell the difference between her being behind the wheel, and him. She experimented with the response of the big boat, moving the wheel to the left.

"Whoa there, lady," Jett said under his breath, and Sadie was unsure if he was directing his comment at her or The Majestic. The yacht dipped sharply. She and Jett stumbled and she scrambled to grab onto something solid to avoid a fall. The wind tore loudly through the sails, reminding Sadie of a massive locomotive chugging over its track.

"I'm sorry!" she yelled.

Jett recovered first. He took hold of the helm and like you would expect from a yacht captain, within a minute, he had the boat righting itself. She stared at him, eyes wide while she worked to get her breathing back to normal. "What? Happened?" she choked out.

He dared to smile at her discomfort. "You turned too abruptly to the starboard and the sails caught too much wind. It's okay. Rookie mistake."

She released her death grip on side of the boat. "Did I do any harm?"

"No. Let's try it again. Are you up to it?"

"Of course." She took a few steps towards him and stood at the helm again.

"Unlike a motor boat, you can't steer anywhere you like. You have to understand what the wind is doing, where it's heading. The wind powers the sailboat. An ill-advised turn of the wheel could, worst case scenario, capsize the boat."

She nodded. Of course, she knew that, but now she had firsthand evidence, and she'd never forget it.

Jett stood behind her and reached his arms over her shoulders, holding onto the wheel along with her. She looked up and behind her with a smile. She felt safe in his arms. Needing to redeem herself, she asked, "So, what would be the correct way to steer this baby?"

With all four of their hands on the helm, and Jett standing directly behind her, they experimented with changing direction. The extent of the wheel's turn and what the boat did in response. If the turn caused the sails to take on too much wind, Jett taught her how to point the sails more into the wind. Once, he instructed her how to release the sheet to let the sail out, while he remained firmly behind the helm. Listening to his shouted instructions, she concentrated on executing properly and observing the response of the boat.

"This is cool," Sadie said, lifting her face up to the sun, closing her eyes and soaking in the warmth. The birds were less populated out this far, but a splash in the ocean caused her to look out about twenty yards, where a dolphin jumped playfully, appearing to smile and wave at them before he dove back underwater. The water was so blue and enticing, she felt like diving in for a swim with the sleek animal.

"Sure is."

"It's a sport that takes a lot of training and knowledge."

"Yeah."

"Your dad gave you quite a gift, both raising you on the water and giving you this boat, huh?"

He didn't respond, and when a long moment of silence passed, Sadie pulled her attention away from the beauty of her surroundings and focused on his face. A crease in his forehead told her he was thinking hard about her last comment.

"I suppose so," he said, and pasted a forced smile on his face. "How about we head back?"

"Sure," she said.

Jett maneuvered the boat in a wide circle and they headed back to the marina. On the return trip, Sadie soaked in the beauty of the water, the sparkle of the sunlight on the waves, the loud squawky seabirds flying overhead, and the strange tightness in her chest when she allowed herself to watch Jett in action. His competence as captain of the ship was on clear display and she had a hard time pulling her eyes away from him. Completely inappropriate, since he was just an old friend and had been nice enough to offer her a ride today. A solitary invitation that she'd been excited to accept, but she was certain it had never been intended to lead to anything else.

Like a romance.

Get your head together, she lectured herself. She had enough going on in her life without messing it up with matters of the heart. She was the one who had never been interested in love or a boyfriend. Love led to disaster, in her experience, and she had way more important things to do.

They returned to the dock, and Jett once again maneuvered the big boat into his slip like it was an effortless exercise. He lowered the sails, secured the boat in its spot, locked everything up and joined her on the pier. He looked down at her with a casual smile. "So?"

"So ... I loved it. Thank you so much. I can't believe what I've been missing all these years by not getting into boating."

He laughed. "You're still young enough. Let me know if you ever want to sail with me again."

Adrenaline flooded her heart. She tried hard to give him a casual response, "I'll do that."

He dropped her off at the gym and before she got out of his truck, she turned to him. "Seriously, that was so much fun. Thank you."

He made a gesture like he was tipping his cap, which he was not wearing, and said, "My pleasure."

Looking down at her seat belt to disconnect it, she was startled when he placed his hand on her arm. His palm warmed her skin and her heartrate skittered. She glanced at him.

"Say, um, what would you think of grabbing some dinner togeth-er?" he asked, his expression unreadable. So unreadable that she had no idea how to interpret the invitation. "I mean, we both worked hard out there, and we could use some nutrition. How about sharing a table with me and letting someone else do the cooking?"

She studied his face and her heart rate slowed again. This did not sound like a date. It did not sound like he was hoping for a romance or a relationship beyond friendship. Good. But just to be safe, she'd better not accept.

"Thanks for thinking of my well-being, Skipper, but I have dinner plans." She hopped out and waved. "You have a good evening now."

She headed for her car, wondering if she'd seen disappointment in his eyes.

~ * ~

Shaw Flynn finished his appointments for the day—his patients exam-ined, vaccinated, stitched up or medicated as needed. He loved work-ing as a large animal veterinarian, and since he was the only one in the Murrells Inlet area, his patients kept him busy. He wouldn't want it any other way. He checked the clock in the pick-up. He had ninety min-utes before meeting Nora for dinner. He wouldn't need all that time to shower and drive to her renovated mansion on the coast of the in-let. He'd use the extra time for an errand that had been weighing on his mind.

He headed toward a strip of stores on Ocean Highway heading north. Not an errand, exactly. That made it sound mundane, or both-ersome even. This job was neither of those things. This job was impor-tant. He was blessed to be able to claim it on his To Do list.

He parked outside a jewelry store and walked in. He navigated to the showcases featuring sparkly stones, leaning close to study them.

"Good evening," said a young blonde woman. "Looking for any-thing in particular?"

"Yes. An engagement ring."

"Congratulations."

He took in a deep breath and let it out. "Thank you. Can you help me figure out which one ...?" He motioned across the broad display case and raised his eyebrows.

"There are a lot to choose from, I'll give you that." She took out a key ring and started picking through the stack of keys before opening the case and bringing out trays of rings. "Do you know what type of ring would strike her fancy?"

"No." Maybe he should've brought Nora. No, he wanted to do this right and surprise her. But maybe, to guide him in the right direction, he should've had a conversation with her. Did she have a preference? If so, she'd never mentioned it. Of course, they'd only just started discussing the subject of marriage and commitment. That night on the south beach on Pawleys Island when she told him she loved him, and they discussed a future together. It was so recent. But so welcome. He wanted to jump on it and take action.

Before she changed her mind?

No, she wouldn't change her mind. They weren't rushing into this. They'd already taken it slowly, gotten to know each other, broken each other's hearts, separated themselves, and finally, started over. That was more than many couples went through in a lifetime, and that history was already behind them. All he was interested in now was what was in front of them.

"Why don't you tell me about your lady and maybe we can figure out what she would like."

A smile formed on his face as he thought about Nora. "She's smart and accomplished. She's beautiful and loving. She is hardworking and ambitious. But she also knows when to change priorities and what's important."

As he said all that, he was looking down at the diamond ring selection, hoping one would miraculously jump up and present itself to him as the right pick. It didn't, however. And in the silence that followed his speech, he turned back to the saleswoman, giving her a curious glance.

"Oh my gosh," she said, wiping tears that had begun to form in her eyes. "That was the sweetest, most loving thing I've ever heard a man say. I hope a man says something like that about me someday."

Shaw chuckled uncomfortably. "Does any of that point me to the right ring?"

The woman shrugged. "Maybe. Does she work with her hands? Do anything that would get them dirty?"

Shaw thought about the times Nora needed to clean out horse stalls, groom and feed the horses, and occasionally ride them. "Sometimes, yeah."

"Okay, so maybe not something overly elaborate." She moved to another tray. "What about a solitaire? Just one diamond, not surrounded by a bunch of others."

Shaw took a look. It was classic, and beautiful. But. "It sits up so high, it might snag on fabric when she arranges dresses."

The woman nodded. "I think I might have just the thing." She moved to the last tray.

Shaw gazed at the solid gold bands inlaid with rows of diamonds. He ran his finger over them. They wouldn't snag on anything or be damaged by manual labor. The saleswoman was right. It was perfect. "I think you're right. Can I bring it back if she hates it?"

She laughed. "Yes, but I have the feeling she's not going to hate it." She pulled the ring out of the display row. "I'll polish it for you and put it in a velvet box."

The thought of a velvet box with a diamond ring in it made his heart beat faster. He'd placed a diamond ring on a woman's finger once before, and it had turned into a calamity. But this was a second chance. This time, he'd picked a quality woman who had the same values, same interests, and same faith in God.

This time, all would be good.

Chapter Three

The morning of the Cannonball Run in Greenville, North Carolina dawned sunny and muggy. May was naturally hot in the Carolinas. Running marathons in chillier weather was preferable to hot weather, but Sadie'd been marathoning for two years. She could do hot; she could do cold. She loved them all.

As she completed her full stretch-out in Jaycee Park, she glanced around, trying to spot other racers in her category and age bracket. There was that Jackie woman who had won the Myrtle Beach Marathon last fall. And there was Tricia, who'd won the Richmond Marathon last summer in Virginia. Winning her division was something Sadie hadn't accomplished. Yet. But she would. Just give her time. Maybe today was her day.

She was feeling strong. Training for her sixth marathon had been much easier than training for her first. She stayed in shape between races, so her training wasn't intended to prepare her for a single day, and then she'd just stop. She enjoyed physical fitness and pushing her body to its limits and thrilling over the adrenaline surging through her. The end goal was to maintain energy to finish strong.

A friend from her gym had accompanied her to the race today. She glanced over at Cindy, stretching alongside of her. "How do you feel?" Sadie asked her.

Cindy shook her head. "I rolled an ankle about two weeks ago and it's still sore."

"Oh, I'm so sorry. Is it wrapped?"

"Yeah. I'm pretty sure I'll finish, but I don't think it'll be a competitive time. Don't wait for me." Cindy looked over and caught Sadie's gaze. "As if you would." She chuckled.

Sadie laughed too. "No, I mean, we both go at our own pace, but I don't want you to be hurt and need some help and I'm ahead, unaware."

Cindy shrugged. "Don't worry about me. The race offers help if I need it. The way I feel today, I'm sure my mind will be churning through all the items on my To Do list. You keep your mind focused on making your best time. With the way you've been kicking butt in training, if you trim a minute or two off, you'd be on the winners' podium."

A surge of excitement flowed through Sadie's chest. That was the goal. A bronze medal in her category, Female Ages 20 to 29. Of course, everyone in her division was young, healthy and fit. But someone had to win. Why not her?

She shook out her legs and went over to Cindy. She wrapped an arm around her friend's shoulders and pulled her in for a loose hug. "Thanks, buddy. Best of luck today. See you at the finish line."

Sadie walked to the start to join the group of runners who had already gathered there. The race would have a gradual shotgun start, to avoid congestion on the route and allow achievement of best time. Her bib was marked with her start time for accurate measurement. Shaking out her arms and legs, breathing deep, she took a moment to close her eyes and pray like she'd done before every other race. Not only did she like to call on the strength and power of the Almighty when she raced, but now that it was a successful habit, she didn't want to jinx herself by skipping it in her warm-up activities.

Lord, please be with me every step over the next twenty-six miles. Give me strength, help me keep moving forward and making wise decisions. I thank you for my body and the ability you've given me to do what I love. Amen.

The first shotgun went off, setting off the start of about a hundred runners. The remaining runners moved forward, positioning themselves for their start. The timer clicked down three minutes. Sadie maneuvered as best she could to the front of the crowd, so she wouldn't be fighting foot traffic at the outset.

The gun went off and Sadie darted forward. She knew what her best pace would be to reach her goal, because she'd done it so many times. Although this was mainly a physical game, it was a mental one too. She needed to keep thinking and strategizing and carrying out her plan as she ran.

The first five miles were, in some ways, the hardest of the entire race. She struggled to settle in, to find her position among the other runners. She knew that to achieve the adrenaline rush of crossing the finish line, she'd need to put in a lot of effort and expect pain. Her mind drifted. Why was she spending half the day doing this, when she had other tasks she needed to complete at home?

A strict internal talking-to was warranted. This race was the most important thing she had to do all day. She had to shove those other things out of her mind. They'd still be waiting for her when she returned home. She only had one chance to accomplish her goal of placing in this race. She needed to be present in the moment, *every* moment for the next several hours.

She purposely took notice of the beauty of the route. Greenville was a charming town nestled into the foothills of the Smoky Mountains, and the route ran through scenic Jaycee Park before launching out into highways winding through the hills and past the historic Biltmore Hotel. *Look,* she told herself, *enjoy, immerse.*

At mile six, she routed slightly off the road to the checkpoint tent. She held out her hand and connected with a cup of water from race volunteers, still in flight. Only a second or two delay, but she needed the hydration. She gulped four or five mouthfuls, then poured the rest of it down the back of her neck. She threw the cup, knowing a clean up crew would be coming along to sweep it up, and she kept running.

At the ten-mile checkpoint, she recognized her familiar love/hate relationship with running marathons. On the love side, she'd hit the double digits. She had endured ten miles and was well into the race. On the hate side, she knew she had lots of enduring left to do. She was doing well from a mental endurance standpoint, but she struggled, trying to ignore the physical pain. Legs had to learn to run tired. The more she ran, the less it hurt. Marathon training was all about teaching your body to conquer this unconceivable distance – time and time again.

The training also taught her how to recognize the difference between her body's gripes. This time she decided to take care of her right shoe which she'd tied a little too tight. It was cutting into her circulation, causing her foot to go numb. She routed to the side, came to a complete stop, leaned over and loosened the laces. She shook her foot out and as the blood started flowing properly again, she re-tied and took off. How much time would she have to make up for that adjustment? She increased her speed to accommodate.

At the thirteen-mile point, a cheerful group of spectators yelled and held up signs, "Half way there!" They yelled and clapped. "Keep going! You're doing great!" Sadie grinned. She felt great now. No problems, now that her foot was back to normal. She wondered for a moment how Cindy was doing and said a quick prayer that her friend would be fine. She glanced at the stopwatch on her wrist. Her goal was always to be at two hours or less at the thirteen-mile mark and strive for the negative split: run the second half faster than the first half. She gave a grim smile when she saw her time: one hour, fifty-six minutes. That marked the best thirteen-mile time she'd ever had.

Somewhere between nineteen and twenty, Sadie started to drag. Her mind was playing games with her. *You can't do this. What made you think you could do this again? You're going to fail.* The urge to break her pace and walk was overwhelming. But experience was the best teacher. She refused to panic because this was her pattern. She expected to drag about this point. She unzipped the front pocket of the pack she had strapped around her waist and pulled out an energy bar, designed to provide a quick boost of sugar. It was sized to consume in about four bites, and she concentrated on biting the proper amount, chewing thoroughly and swallowing. At the next water point she'd make sure she grabbed a cup and drank eight ounces to wash it down and prevent her stomach from revolting.

And she pulled another strategy out, too. A memory of her fitness coach, Jett Martin, running beside her while she was training for her first marathon two years ago. "Words are powerful," he'd told her. "Talk to yourself and believe what you're saying."

"What should I say?" she'd asked him, huffing and puffing at the twenty-mile mark, desperate to quit. She wasn't sure at that time if she believed it. It seemed too simple, too hokey.

Running strong beside her, he said, "I've come this far, how much more can I go? One more mile, then one more. How far can I go?"

She'd nodded, concentrating on his words instead of the pain in her chest, in her feet, in her back.

"Run with purpose, Sadie," Jett had said. "You're in charge of your race. No one can tell you that you can't do this. Prove it to yourself. You *can* do this."

Just as she had two years ago during that training race with Jett, she repeated the words to herself now. This was a once in a lifetime experience and she wouldn't waste it. Yes, she'd run another marathon, God willing. But she would never run *this* marathon again, on *this* course, on *this* day. Then she remembered another mantra her father told her when she left for every race: "Just go have fun."

She tilted her head back and laughed joyfully. "Just have fun!" she shouted, drawing some amused stares from the racers around her. "We think this is fun?" They chuckled, and she powered on.

At twenty-four miles, she was breezing. Her energy had returned, and she was close enough to the end that pure excitement was carrying her through. Her shoulders ached, her feet hurt from a blister on her right big toe, but her breathing and cardio were fine, and her legs were hanging in there. Nothing that she needed to worry about now.

With the finish line approaching, she reached deep inside her and wondered if she had a last burst of strength to cross it in style. Yes, she thought she did. She waited till the last quarter mile and increased her pace. Steaming over the finish line, she lifted her arms out like airplane wings. Spectators clapped and cheered. Sadie smiled and made eye contact with as many people as she could. She broke her pace to a walk and headed for an open space in the park to walk slow laps, to gradually prepare her body to stop. As she walked, careful not to trip or fall, she said a prayer of thanksgiving in her head.

When she'd finished her cool down she wandered over to the results board. The race was still in progress, so she couldn't tell where she'd finished. But she did know one thing: she'd beaten her personal best time. She'd run the marathon in three hours and fifty-four minutes. Excitement welled inside her, along with hope that her time would be enough to get on the podium.

She headed over to the food trucks and bought herself a grilled chicken sandwich. When she'd finished it, she wandered back and bumped into Cindy, who had finished the race, with a slower time than normal due to her bum ankle.

"Hey, I finished. That was my goal today," Cindy said.

"Great. Keep nursing that ankle and the next time you can improve your time."

All that was left now was waiting for the placement announcements.

~ * ~

Jett got off work at the gym at three. Changing into swim trunks and a tank shirt, he jumped into his truck and headed for the marina. He had repairs to do on the yacht. Rather, he'd call them renovations. Or enhancements. There were always renovations to do. A sailing yacht was never 100% perfect. Buffing down the rough spots from the hull, re-applying the gelcoat to a glossy finish, the occasional patching job when waves were particularly rough and threw the ship around, or into an obstruction.

Then there was the engine. He hadn't been a mechanic till he'd received this vessel from his dad. The boat was over thirty years old, and especially on long trips or demanding races, the engine was always moaning and groaning over something. After three years of performing his own mechanical work, he couldn't imagine the engine could come up with an issue that he hadn't already figured out.

And the sails. A sailboat with faulty sails was a disaster. Sails were fragile compared to the engine and hull and required extra care. Rinsing the sails with fresh water and drying them thoroughly before storage to prevent mildew. Removing stains caused by oil, rust or grease to maximize the lifetime of the expensive sails. Patching minor tears.

In short, the maintenance of a high-performance sailing yacht could take up all the hours in his day, and that was before he even took the boat out in the water.

He parked at the Crazy Sisters marina and hopped out of the truck. He circled to the open bed, pulled out his tool chest and made his way to the wooden boardwalk. In the slip next to The Majestic's, his neighbor was visible just below surface in his cabin. He waved. "Hey Jett," he called, and his head disappeared below deck.

"Hey Mark," Jett replied and set his heavy trunk on the dock. Mark was probably ten years older than Jett, and had started the whole marriage, career and family part of his life. He probably didn't have leisure for the time-consuming hobby of yacht sailing, but Jett had to admire the fact that he still made it a priority.

Mark popped back into view. "You taking her out today?"

Jett gazed at the yacht, thought about it, then shook his head. "Nah, I've got some work to do on her. First the engine. Then, if it's not dark, I could work on these sails."

Mark laughed. "You sure give her the tender loving care, dude."

"Well, I don't have a girlfriend, so I'm forced to shower the TLC on this beautiful creation."

Mark picked up a mop and started pushing it over the floor of his cabin. "I don't know, I saw you and a young lady sail off last week together."

Jett frowned, putting his memory to the test. "Oh, yeah, Sadie." Sadie Flynn, who spent a perfectly fun afternoon with him on the boat, got his imagination running about how awesome she would be to date, and then turned him down flat when he'd asked her out. Yeah, that Sadie.

"Okay. Sadie seemed like a good prospect, and you could impress her with your sailing expertise."

Jett chuckled, an attempt to whitewash over the stab of her rejection in his heart. "She's a pretty girl all right, but we're just friends. In fact, she was a client of mine a few years ago."

"Oh. Could get weird then, huh?"

Jett shrugged. "Well, not necessarily. I mean, I'm not on her payroll currently."

Mark gave him an eyebrows-up look. "Something to think about."

Jett pulled out a wrench and a screwdriver and boarded his boat, making his way to the engine compartment. "I've got enough to think about with my race coming up."

Mark stopped what he was doing. "Tell me. Where are you racing?"

Jett glanced over at him. Mark's attention was lasered on him. The poor guy tended to live life vicariously through Jett, at least when it came to sailing. Mark's life was much fuller with a big-time career, doing whatever he did in the office, a wife and kids, paying all the bills and saving for his kids' college. Jett's was much simpler. But Jett knew Mark would be making the yacht racing circuit if he could.

Jett laid his tools down to fill his slip neighbor in. "I've had my eye on a long-distance race for a long time, Bermuda Newport. It appeals to me because it finishes in Bermuda, which of course, is just off the Carolina coast."

"Yeah, it's prestigious too. I've heard of Bermuda Newport. It starts in Rhode Island, right?"

"Yep. It provides open sea sailing, and it's a multi-day race."

"How many days?"

"Well," Jett said and scratched his jaw, "the winners take between four and five days."

Mark chuckled. "What about the non-winners?"

Jett grinned. "They could be out there six, seven sometimes." He shook his head, hoping he wouldn't be one of those unlucky souls. "This is the first year they're opening a single-handed division. Up till this year, the race only allowed teams."

"That won't be easy."

Jett got back on his feet, ready to work on the engine. "Challenge is what makes it worthwhile."

"True that. I wish you the best, man. When do you leave?"

"About three weeks. Thanks." He returned to the engine hatch and started his work. He wasn't going to get into it with Mark, but he'd specifically selected the Newport Bermuda race because of its challenge and length, because he had a vested interest in proving that his ship could perform well in the prestigious race. Many eyes would be upon his every move and his results, and this was his chance to prove his concept.

He hoped this race would be the start of a whole new life for him beyond his wildest dreams. Either that, or it could be a miserable failure. Only time would tell.

~ * ~

"Racers, please make your way to the podium for the announcements of the top three placers in each division."

Sadie pulled to her feet. Glancing around, she noticed that a vast majority of the runners had taken off. She would've too, if she wasn't in the running for a medal. She had no idea if she'd placed fast enough to score, but she wasn't about to leave before she found out.

Cindy grabbed her hand and squeezed it. "Good luck," she said softly.

An anxious breath tripped down Sadie's throat. "Thanks."

It was a simple set up with three platforms, the highest one in the middle, lower ones on each side. A microphone stand and a man with a clipboard.

"Ladies first," the man announced into the microphone. Sadie turned to Cindy and gave her a grim expression. *Here goes.*

"In the category of Female, ages fourteen to nineteen, we will begin with the winner of the bronze."

Sadie listened and clapped for each one and watched while each winner bounded up to the platform and jumped onto their appropriate one. The runner bent forward at the waist while a race official placed the medal around their neck, and then she straightened, waving and smiling at the cheering crowd. Sadie didn't have long to wait until she got her answer.

"In the category of Female, ages twenty to twenty-nine, we will begin with the winner of the bronze medal." He pulled the microphone away from his face and flipped the page on his clipboard. Sadie cringed at the unexpected amplified sound.

"With a time of three hours, fifty-four minutes and twelve seconds ..."

Sadie's brain raced with numbers. Wasn't that her time? Or was she a few seconds slower? Had she missed the bronze by two seconds?

"Sadie Flynn of Murrells Inlet, South Carolina."

Cindy screamed beside her and patted her shoulder. Sadie froze as dizziness swept over her. "Get up there, girl! Go get your medal!"

Sadie stumbled forward, and somehow made it up to the podium and received the medal around her neck. It was lucky each winner wasn't expected to give an acceptance speech because her tongue was tied, and she had no idea what to say. But she waved and smiled and waited till her competitors joined her on their own podiums. Turning her head, she saw familiar faces: Tricia had come in first, and Jackie had the second-place spot. She smiled when she realized the fine company she was in. These ladies were always in the top three. This was her first time joining them.

She stepped off the podium and Tricia came her way. "Congratulations on your bronze."

Sadie smiled. She was as starstruck as if Jennifer Lawrence had just spoken to her. "Thanks. And congrats on your gold."

Cindy approached her. "You ready to get going?"

"Yep." They walked back to the car. It had been an awesome day. She'd run well, she'd made a personal best, and she'd won a medal. What could be better?

Chapter Four

Jett's cell buzzed on the table next to him.

Call me.

His father's text sent a surge of anxiety down his esophagus. Then he took a deep breath. His father had no power over him anymore. The brusque text didn't necessarily mean he was angry. That was just his way of communicating.

Jett set the phone on the table and tried to concentrate on the relaxing evening of TV he'd planned for tonight. But the magnetic pull of his father's message continued to draw his attention away.

Might as well get it over with. He pulled up the number and hit Send.

"You're competing in the Newport Bermuda?" his father's voice boomed over the little device. No 'hello. No 'thanks for calling, son.' Why would his dad engage in polite small talk when he wanted something from Jett?

"Yes," Jett responded and waited to hear what problem his father had with this. Because that was the only time he heard from Dad, now that he was an adult. When his father was angry or irritated by him or wanted to dispense advice about how he should change the way he was living his life.

A derisive scoff came over the connection. "Why waste your money on that race, son? You really think you have a chance at competing?"

A bubble of a giggle came to Jett's lips and he tamped it down. *Tell me what you really think, Pops.* Their relationship had always been like this. His father had always disapproved of him. Jett had never lived up to the expectations Cameron Martin had set for him, never reached the bar. Once he'd hit the age of eighteen, when society felt he was an adult, he'd removed himself from his father's care. He became completely independent. He didn't ask for anything. In his mind, that gave him the freedom to live life his own way, without his father's input.

Too bad his dad didn't see it that way.

"I've had my eye on this race for a while, Dad. I'll throw myself out there and see how it goes."

"That's the problem with you, son. That's a perfect strategy for your entire life, isn't it? Throw yourself out there and see how it goes. No planning, no preparing, no knowing ahead of time if you can even be successful."

Jett clamped his lips shut and dulled his senses to his father's familiar tirade. *Yes, Dad, I know you're disappointed in me. Yes, Dad, I know you had a different plan for me. Let it go.*

When the voice over the line had finished droning, Jett said, "As always, nice talking to you." He carefully kept the sarcasm out of his tone, but he knew his word choice alone would be enough to ignite his father's anger.

"So, I can't talk you into withdrawing from the race?"

"Why would I do that?" Wait, had he missed crucial information while he was tuning out?

"Because I'm competing in that race, too."

Interesting. Two Martins competing in the same race. His father, with a lifetime more experience than him, a much more expensive, glossy, modern boat, and Jett, with Daddy's leftovers. Why would his father want to prevent Jett from competing against him? Could it possibly be that he thought Jett could beat him? Or, more likely, was he ashamed of Jett and didn't want him to tarnish the family name? "What category are you enrolled in?"

"Double-handed crew."

"Ahh, too bad, Dad. I'm in the single-handed division."

His father paused. "Jett, where's your head? Did you even do your homework? This is so like you. This race doesn't offer a single-handed race."

Jett couldn't help the gleeful smile that covered his face, the same one he got whenever his dad was wrong. "They're adding a single-handed division this year, Dad. I'll be in it."

Jett let the line go quiet for a few seconds. It was unusual for his father to be speechless. "Better go, Dad. See you in Newport." And he broke the connection before his dad could say another word.

~ * ~

"Ten more, then you're done," Jett said to his client, a young man who was reclined on a weight bench, executing on the custom work out plan Jett had created for him. Rich was a football player at a local college and wanted to make sure he stayed in decent shape in the off-season. Jett kept an eye on Rich as he lifted. The phone in his pocket vibrated, since he'd turned the ringer off. He pulled it out of his pocket and glanced at the caller. "Okay, Rich, let's end it there. I've got to get this."

Rich nodded and sat, shaking out his arms.

"Hit the shower. Good job today," said Jett, then connected the call. "Hey Mason. How are you today?"

"I'm good. And you are going to be good when you hear the awesome opportunity I have for you."

Jett instinctively recoiled from the 'O word.' Often, an 'opportunity' could mean lots of work with little to no result. "Okay, what's this opportunity?"

"I finagled something that you're going to like. Sailtone is attending a boat showcase event in Myrtle Beach. It starts tomorrow night. We've got representatives from all our divisions going – Development, Finance and Manufacturing. Right down the street from you, right?"

"Yeah. Myrtle Beach is only a dozen miles away," Jett said.

"Since the showcase doesn't start until tomorrow evening, and I'll have the big guns here, and you're right down the street, I scheduled a meeting. With you." Mason sounded positively gleeful.

"Me?" Jett's heart started to pound.

"Yeah. You can do a demo, talk about your product, get them on board."

Jett's mouth dropped open. He wasn't a salesman. And he wasn't a public speaker. He was a sailor, and as of recently, an inventor of a product that could help sailors. But he needed to get it picked up by a big company with funds and a manufacturing division so he could get it out to the sailing world.

A big company like Sailtone.

"Mason, I'm awful at stuff like that. You're the talker. Why don't you do the demo and the presentation, and I'll be there to answer technical questions?"

"They've heard me talk about your sunscreen lotion for sails. They are intrigued and think it could fill a big gap in the sailing industry. But they're not completely on board yet. Maybe you can be the swing. Turn on your charm and your expertise and maybe they'll buy into it."

Jett thought for a moment. He'd be an idiot to turn down this chance, even if it made him uncomfortable. So far, Mason was the only contact person he'd formed a relationship with at Sailtone, the only one who'd heard his pitch. It wouldn't hurt to have big wigs from Finance and Manufacturing hear about his proposed invention. If Sailtone were to finally sign on to it, they'd all have to be committed.

"Okay. Tell me when and where."

"Yeah, there you go, man!" Mason gave him the details and Jett hung up, his stomach in knots. *Guess I'll be spending tonight coming up with a sales presentation.*

After four evening hours of work and a restless night, Jett headed to the gym for a partial work day. He was scheduled to meet Mason and his Sailtone cronies at their hotel in Myrtle Beach late in the afternoon. Mason had reserved a small conference room for his presentation. After making his way through several clients' workouts, Jett left with plenty of time to spare, expecting the worst of Myrtle Beach traffic.

He walked into the hotel with ten minutes to spare, carrying a backpack filled with items he needed for the presentation. Mason was standing in the lobby. He held out his hand and shook Jett's vigorously. "Hey, buddy, good to see you."

"Yeah, it's been a while." He'd only met Mason once in person, close to a year ago, when Sailtone had offered a targeted Open House in their headquarters in St. Petersburg, Florida. They'd advertised in the major sailing magazines that they were looking to invest in new products to aid the sailing and yachting industries. Amateur inventors with an idea were invited to apply for an audience with Sailtone's Research and Development department.

The promotion had come at an excellent time for Jett, who had been hemming and hawing over his invention for quite some time: wondering if he had something useful, or if anyone else would think it was useful besides him. He figured this was the chance to get some answers. He'd applied and was rewarded with a meeting in person with Mason. After selling Mason on the idea, his next step was applying for the patent, which he'd completed. Although Mason had been great to work with, he was unable to take the invention any farther along in the company unless he could sell the idea to others. A budget had to be allocated and approved, and the proper priority had to be established in Manufacturing to start working on it.

Jett tugged on his necktie. He'd thrown in on at the last moment before walking out the door because he figured everyone else in the room would be wearing one. Regretting it because it choked him, he wondered if he should've just gone with his normal attire of shorts and t-shirt rather than this stuffy suit.

"Okay, this way, man," Mason said, gesturing with one hand and resting the other on Jett's back. Jett estimated Mason to be younger than him, probably working his first good job out of college, trying to make a mark. Well, if this presentation went well and the big guns bought into his sunscreen lotion for sails idea, it would mean a big break for them both.

They walked down a hallway and into a conference room. Two men and a woman sat there, chatting comfortably with each other. Jett gasped silently when he noticed they were all dressed in deck clothes: shorts and polo shirts.

"I'd like to introduce one of our patented inventors, Jett Martin."

Jett resisted the urge to roll his eyes. Yes, it was true, but he sure didn't think of himself that way. He held up a hand and gave a lame wave. "Hi, everyone."

"I'll make introductions," Mason continued. He gestured to a man who had to be in his late fifties, with salt and pepper hair and about forty extra pounds residing around his waist. "This is our Chief Financial Officer, Fred Romine. He, of course, controls the checkbook."

Jett forced a smile and walked closer to shake the man's hand. "Nice to meet you." The CFO nodded.

"And this is Margaret Foster. She is the head of our Manufacturing division."

Ms. Foster was at least a decade younger than Mr. Romine, a pretty brunette who looked like she kept in shape. "Hi," he said, dipping his head toward her and shaking her hand.

"And this is my colleague in Research and Development, Brian Boyster. He's along for the ride today."

"Nice to meet you," Jett said, with one more handshake. Brian smiled. He was the youngest of the four and Jett figured Mason was mentoring him.

Mason continued, "As I mentioned to you all, Jett Martin's invention was selected last year in the Trendsetters promotion, and it is now patented. Like so many others, he's competing to get his idea into our process stream. I've been working with Jett for a year and I think he's really got something here that will be useful to our customers. Since we're right in his backyard today, I asked him to stop by and talk to you about it. Jett?" Mason turned to him with a big smile. "All yours."

Jett cleared his throat. "Thanks, Mason. I really appreciate the chance to talk to you all today. But before I do, let me take care of one thing." He removed his suit jacket and made a show of loosening his tie before pulling it off. The others chuckled. "Now, I feel a little better."

He reached into his backpack and pulled out his laptop. Within a minute, he'd powered it on, pulled up his Powerpoint presentation and connected it to the projector so they could follow along on the screen. The initial image was a broad shot photo of The Majestic.

"This is my boat. It's a Warwick Allegro, thirty-three-foot sailing yacht. Her sails when fully extended reach about fifty feet high. She's over thirty years old, and I do all the work on her myself to make sure she's in peak sailing and racing condition. That's The Majestic." He paused and let the others soak in her beauty, as well as all the statistics he'd just thrown at them.

"I enjoy the multi-day high seas racing competitions. They put both the vessel and its captain through their paces. To heighten the excitement, I only race single-handed." He glanced at the observers and they nodded, a few raising their eyebrows in appreciation.

"It takes a lot of maintenance to care for a girl like her. I'm constantly working on the engine and deck to take care of problems. But the thing I'm most careful about are the sails. Surveys taken of experienced yacht racers over the last decade have identified the biggest weakness of long-distance sailboat races. Do you know what it is?"

The three consulted with each other then Fred looked at him and shrugged. "Tears in the sails?"

Jett smiled. "That's a good guess, especially on high wind days when those sails are flapping up a storm. But no. The biggest weakness of long-distance sailboat races is UV exposure damage to the sails. Races often take place in the hot weather months, and they span several days. UV exposure can literally destroy your sails and they have to be replaced ... a very expensive solution ... either between races, or if absolutely necessary, in the midst of a race. That's a perfect way to ruin your day."

They chuckled, and Jett started to relax, feeling comfortable with the topic and the reception he was receiving.

"My idea was to create a formula, a sunscreen, if you will, to rub into the sail fabric and remedy this problem. Hey, we know how to prevent sunburn on human skin by using UV protection, right? I've just adjusted that recipe to provide UV protection to the synthetic fibers of the sailcloth." He advanced to the next picture in his presentation. "This is a photo of a sailboat whose sails have been rotted by sun damage." He pointed. "You see how the sail's fabric is inconsistent? There are healthy, thick sections, and damaged, thin sections. Up here the thin sections have actually torn." He moved on to another photo of The Majestic. "I treat The Majestic's sails with my sunscreen prototype every week, and as you can see, the sails look brand new." He clicked to the next picture, a close-up of the sailcloth. "No thin spots, no tears, no problems that would prevent me from sailing her at high speeds through an entire multi-day competition."

He reached into his backpack and pulled out a small tub of his lotion as well as a foot-long square of sailcloth. Using his fingers, he rubbed a glob of the lotion into the sailcloth, massaging it in so it went from thick, to wet to completely absorbed. "As you can see, once the lotion is absorbed into the sail, you see no traces of it. But rest assured, it's in there, doing its job, protecting the sail from the sun's harmful rays and allowing the captain to forget about it and worry about the next thing."

Margaret spoke up. "But how are you going to rub lotion over the entire sail? You said yourself they're fifty feet high."

"Yes. When I do my weekly applications, I use a combination of my hands and this roller." He pulled out a hand-held roller, sort of like a rolling pin that bakers would use in the kitchen. "It's a fairly time-consuming job, but I do it because it's effective and gets results."

Mason jumped to his feet. "And if we agree to move this product forward to Manufacturing, we would consider some alternative types of application methods for our customers. Very good point, Margaret." He nodded his approval to her.

Jett handed the sailcloth sample to Margaret, who examined it and passed it to her colleagues. "That's all I have. Do you have any questions I can answer?" *Or, try to answer.*

Fred looked up from the fabric. "What's the investment you're looking for?"

Jett glanced over at Mason, who jumped in to answer. "Fred, great question. We think we can get an initial offering of the lotion manufactured and on the market for two million dollars."

Jett's stomach clenched internally. He stared at Fred, who jotted something on a piece of paper. "Two million initially," the businessman repeated. "Then what?"

Mason reached for a short stack of papers he'd set on the table in front of him. "We estimated that it will be profitable eighteen months in. So, upfront costs for packaging and advertising. Twenty percent?"

Fred nodded and returned to his paper. He looked up. "I'm good." He placed his pen down.

Jett had no idea what it meant that Fred was good, but figured it was a more positive indicator than Fred being bad.

"Margaret?" Mason said.

Margaret looked thoughtful, then said. "Jett, you've said this is an aid for racing ships. What about just regular leisure sailboats?"

"Yes, absolutely. All sails would benefit from UV exposure protection. But my main focus is competitive racing."

"What is your record as a competitive racer? How successful are you?"

Jett knew the statistics without looking it up. "I've placed gold in two major races, silver in five and bronze in one."

Margaret tapped her fingers on the table. "I'm thinking of making our support contingent on a Top 3 finish in an upcoming race. A 'Put your money where your mouth is' approach."

Jett went silent and stared at Margaret for a moment. He wondered how common this approach was. He'd have to ask Mason later.

Mason said, "Margaret, so you're saying if Jett places in the Top 3 in his next race, we commit to sponsoring the project and moving into production?"

"Yes." Margaret blinked and gave a small smile.

"And," Jett blurted, caught himself, then went on, "If I place fourth or lower, you walk away?"

"No, not necessarily," Margaret said. "Our project lists are jam-packed and it's usually a challenge to slip in a new one without finishing others. If we sell this to our executives that you're our trailblazer, not only an inventor, but a sailor, a competitive winner ... I think that would get attention. Might be the leg up we need."

Mason's face exploded with excitement. "How about this idea? We use Jett in our advertising. He'd be our poster boy for the product."

Jett frowned. "Hold on. My winning the race doesn't necessarily endorse the quality of the product. Right?"

Mason patted his shoulder. "It's all part of the corporate game, Jett. These folks are giving you a thumbs up. They like what you have here. They're just brainstorming to come up with a way to make sure it gets through the channels. This is a good thing."

Jett's eyes went wide. Good for Sailtone. A ton of pressure for Jett Martin.

"Do we have an agreement?" Mason said to the room. All the Sail-tone employees murmured their agreement.

"So, if I place in the race, my product gets a contract with you," Jet clarified. "If I don't, we go back to the drawing board."

Fred huffed. "Yes, but honestly it would most likely get buried. Best thing for you to do is to win this big race. When is it, by the way?"

"Less than three weeks."

"Perfect!" yelled Mason. "What could be better?"

The meeting wrap-up, the shaking of the hands and the pats on the back were a blur to Jett. When Mason offered to take him out for a beer, Jett declined. He had to place in the top three of the Newport Bermuda race, and that wouldn't be easy.

Talk about pressure.

~ * ~

Shaw stopped by home late in the afternoon after close to seven hours of veterinary appointments with various clientele across Horry and Georgetown Counties. He took a moment to eat a sandwich in his quiet kitchen. His best thinking was done while sitting at this table. While he ate, he let his mind hover over the issue at hand.

The dark blue velvet box sat in front of him. He opened it while he chewed so he could see the band of encrusted diamonds. The time was right to propose. The question was, how would he do it? He thought back over the dates he'd arranged for the two of them. Dinner at the MarshWalk. Trips to Charleston for dinners in historic restaurants and country music concerts. An evening of dinner theater at the Seaview Inn in Pawleys Island. All successful date nights. Should he plan something like that again? Give her a reason to get gussied up and go somewhere fancy?

As he gazed at the ring, a different idea spoke to him: proposing marriage in a way consistent with what their life would be like together. Their day-in, day-out life would not be about formal dinners and travel.

Sure, they would embark on those outings occasionally, and enjoy them. But the reality of their daily lives as a couple would be different. Continuing the renovations on the big old mansion Nora had inherited from her Aunt Edie. Time spent in the barn taking care of Thunder, the horse at the center of the nonprofit equine therapy venture they'd started together. Giving people the chance at happiness through the simple act of riding a horse: traumatized veterans, disabled children, terminal patients of all ages.

He finished his sandwich and took the plate to the sink. Grabbing the box and placing it in his shirt pocket, he left.

Twenty minutes later, he brought his truck to a halt in front of Nora's barn at Waccamaw Trails, the name of the premiere equestrian center her Aunt Edie had operated in its prime. Ideas about how they could more fully utilize the state-of-the-art facilities Edith had built prior to her death started to tug on his brain, but he pushed them aside. Time for all of that later. Today, he had a priority.

He entered the barn and walked straight to Thunder's stall. The big black gelding walked close, pressing his nose against the bars. Shaw stuck his fingers in and stroked the velvety muzzle. "Hey, buddy. How are you today? Want to stretch those legs?"

He opened the stall and snapped a lead on Thunder's halter. Shaw led him out and took a short walk to the gate of the enclosed pasture. Opening it, he led Thunder in, unsnapped the lead and patted him on the rear. "Have fun."

Thunder lifted his nose and sniffed the air, then ambled away in the opposite direction. He wasn't in a hurry, but within a few minutes, he'd made his way about two hundred yards in the direction of the coastline that took up the far eastern side of Nora's property.

"Hi, handsome."

Her voice caused a trip in Shaw's heartrate. He turned around and smiled.

"I saw your truck when you pulled up," she said.

He took her upper arms and pulled her into an embrace, closing his eyes and breathing in the scent of her hair.

"Well, my goodness," she said, and he could tell she was pleased. "Quite a greeting."

"You smell great." He pulled back and looked into her eyes. "You look great too."

She broke out with a chuckle. "Ah, this old thing?" He turned his attention to what she was wearing. It was, uncharacteristically, a formal business suit. Probably the type of outfit she wore in her past life as a Philadelphia attorney. But definitely not what he was accustomed to seeing her in, in her new life on the coast of South Carolina.

A stab of concern hit him. "Are you going somewhere?" he asked cautiously. He didn't even want to think that maybe her old career in the city had been knocking on her door and she was interested in re-joining that rat race lifestyle.

She grinned. "No. I just got a new shipment of professional clothes in and I couldn't resist trying this one on." She twirled for him, right there in the trimmed grass of the pasture. "What do you think?"

He shrugged. "It looks nice on you. Then again, everything looks nice on you."

She laughed. "It feels like a blast from my past. After a long career of dressing like this every day, I have to admit, this suit feels a bit foreign to me now. I look forward to changing back into shorts and t-shirts, to be honest."

Nora had created an office and wardrobe showroom on the first floor of her mansion and operated a chapter of Dress for Success there. Her clients were women trying to enter the professional workforce. Her services included resume building, mock interviews, and the gift of a professional outfit to wear to interviews. Clothes were donated from all over the country for that purpose.

"I'll go change. You want to come in or are you waiting for Thunder?" She turned and looked at him over her shoulder.

"Actually ... I have something I want to ask you first."

Nora shrugged. "Here? Or can you ask me in the house?"

Shaw looked around. This property was a reflection of the life he and Nora had built together. The mansion, the barn, the horse, their community outreach efforts. Proposing to her here felt right. Before he changed his mind, he went with his gut and reached out a hand.

"Right here." She placed her hand in his palm. "Nora, I love you. I love the life we've already built, but I'm excited about our future, waiting on the horizon. You've shown me what true love is and I want more."

She brought her free hand up to her lips.

He bent his leg and knelt on one knee. "You are truly the woman I've needed my whole life. True love is worth waiting for. So, my love, my Nora, will you marry me?"

She didn't speak right away, but he could tell from her face that she would say yes, eventually. Her eyes welled with tears that dropped on her cheeks. The one hand that was resting in his, squeezed tight. She'd waited a long time for this, as well as he.

"Yes. Yes, Shaw. I will marry you." She pulled him up to his full height and into a kiss.

When they parted, he pulled the box out of his shirt pocket, opened it and faced it toward her. All fear that it wouldn't be what she wanted departed when he saw her expression, gazing at it. Then her words confirmed it. "Oh Shaw, it's stunning."

He tugged it out of its slot. "I went with this because I thought it fit our lifestyle. We can always go with something else if you don't like it."

She gave him a comical look of disbelief. "Don't like it?" She held out her left hand, her ring finger extended. "Slide it on there."

He laughed with relief. He slid the ring on her finger. It was a perfect fit. She positioned it so she could study and admire it. Then she said, "I love it. I'm never taking it off."

He pulled her close for another kiss, his heart pounding with joy. He was a man in his late forties with an established career; he was a widower and a father. But in some ways, his life started now. This instant. The moment he finally found love.

Chapter Five

"The order of stages of bone fracture healing is formation of a hematoma, formation of a fibrocartilaginous callous, formation of a bony callous, and, finally, bone remodeling."

Sadie tapped notes into her tablet as her professor spoke.

"We will be focusing on the first two today, and the second two tomorrow."

School had been back in session for a week, and usually Sadie had absolutely no problem gluing her attention to the lessons. After all, being a registered nurse was her life's dream, and this information was vital. But so far this semester, she'd struggled with her attention span.

Placing third in the marathon last weekend had been such a thrill. Her mind kept running over and over the moment when her name had been announced, and she'd climbed her weary legs up onto the podium amidst applause.

Her next marathon was eight weeks away in Virginia. State number seven of her fifty state quest. But she was also thinking about other challenges besides marathon running. And school.

Sailing the big yacht with Jett had unleashed a desire in her. She wanted to try new things, push herself to perform sports she'd never tried before. Last night, she had researched some extreme adventure sports on the internet. After running through zip lining and rock climbing, she'd stumbled onto what could be the most extreme of all extreme sports: skydiving.

The thought of traveling up into the air in a small plane, strapping on a parachute and jumping out, exhilarated her. Little training was needed for tandem skydiving, strapped to an instructor. But she didn't want to stop there. She wanted to do solo skydiving. For that, a few weeks of classroom training was required, viewing some videos and a series of freefall dives before getting certified. It was something she could do while simultaneously pursuing her marathon goals.

She dragged her attention back to the instructor. He was now discussing the cartilage surrounding a bone fracture. She had missed at least eight minutes of lecture while daydreaming. What was wrong with her? She typed notes as he spoke, trying to get back into the groove of listening. She could compare notes later with a classmate and recover what she'd missed.

But twenty minutes later her mind was drifting again. Way off topic. But this time it wasn't about skydiving or long-distance running.

Her mind had pulled up a visual of Jett Martin. His tanned, smiling face, his white smile, cappuccino-colored eyes and his scruffy hair, brown with sun-bronzed highlights on the tips. He was laughing, as he did more generally than not. He was an easy-going person, so casual and laid back. The direct opposite of her. But she had learned recently, he wasn't happy-go-lucky all the time. He had big goals. He was a competitive yacht racer with ambitions to win prestigious races.

In addition to his physical attributes, she had to admit that his aspiration to win races was the thing she found most attractive about him.

She let her mind settle on that unexpected thought, and then shook her head, cleared her throat and tore her thoughts away from Jett Martin. Back to fracture care, where it should be. She wondered, not for the first time, what was wrong with her. Distracted from class? Thinking instead about skydiving, and God forbid, a potential romance?

No. This was not like her. Her number one priority was her nursing education. Number two was her sporting endeavors. Love didn't even fall into the top three. Or the top ten, for that matter. She had no time for love. She had no interest in building a romantic relationship. Look what her parents had gone through.

Which just proved to Sadie that you absolutely never knew. Your heart could be heading you into a direction that was one hundred percent wrong. You couldn't trust that your heart knew what was right. So, a young woman who had goals and dreams and aspirations needed to stay away from romance. She could befriend men. She could learn from men.

But she would never allow herself to fall in love with one. Period.

She started typing again, something about the type of material of a plaster cast, and how to best form it to encourage healing.

And definitely not with a guy like Jett Martin. No.

~ * ~

"Tropical Storm Cynthia is now predicted to hit Myrtle Beach shores at seven o'clock this evening. Fortunately, there are no indications this storm will be upgraded to a hurricane, however, it will be a strong storm with rain and wind, resulting in moderate storm surges, so residents of the area are encouraged to stay inside tonight. Batten down the hatches, and of course, if you own a boat, either secure it tightly in its slip, or better yet, store it inside for the course of the storm."

Jett glanced at the TV and pulled his frozen dinner out of the microwave. An hour till the storm was anticipated to hit shore. Just in time to eat a quick dinner and get to the slip.

This storm could not have come at a better time.

He drove to the pier, parked in the lot and got out of his truck. Several boat owners scattered across the dock, making storm preparations to minimize damage to their vessels. He greeted several of them as he made his way to his own. Mark, his next-door slip neighbor, was busy strapping down his boat more securely.

"Hey, Jett. I was wondering what your plans were for your sailboat. You got a place to take it out of the storm? I tried to get a spot inside for my wakeboard boat, but they're full. Of course, yours in a lot bigger than mine."

The sky was darkening, and the wind had already picked up. The waves were more choppy than normal, and Jett was having a hard time hearing the conversation without shouting. His concern was how much to tell Mark. If he told him the truth, his well-meaning neighbor would try to talk him out of it. And he didn't have time to deal with that. He settled on, "No, I think it'll be okay."

Mark finished his preparations and wiped his brow. "You're kind of cutting it close, aren't you?" he said with a nervous chuckle. "We've known about this storm for four days and you're just now coming out to tie it up?" He crossed the separating strip of dock and came closer to Jett. Mark watched him for a moment. "What ... what are you doing there, bud?"

Jett stopped working. Mark had noticed that instead of tightening the lines, the anchors, and the sails, Jett was doing the opposite. "Okay, listen. I know what I'm doing."

"You're going out in this storm?" Mark's face scrunched with concern and Jett knew the man thought he was crazy.

Jett continued his preparations. "Look, I don't have time to discuss it right now, because, like you said, I have a tropical storm waiting for me. But just to put your mind at ease I'm using this storm as a training opportunity."

"A what?"

"You know I have that long-distance race in a couple of weeks, right? Newport, Rhode Island to Bermuda."

"Yeah," Mark said dubiously.

"They don't cancel those races due to weather. Unless it's a categorized hurricane, the race goes on. So, I want to train in a tropical storm. Practice makes perfect, right?"

Mark studied his face for a moment and then shook his head. "Yeah but, by yourself? At night? In a tropical storm? Seems crazy, dude."

Jett suppressed a chuckle. Sometimes yacht racing could be considered crazy. The fact that he didn't consider it that way, meant that he was well-suited for the sport. Other people saw a tropical storm and they stayed far away from the ocean. He saw a tropical storm, and he couldn't make it to the boat fast enough to get out there.

"I'll be fine. Thanks for your concern, though." He boarded the boat, hoping his explanation would put an end to the conversation.

Mark walked closer, facing him from the dock. "What will you do if you need help? Who will you call?"

Jett couldn't imagine anything happening that he couldn't handle himself. He wasn't going out that deep, and only planned a two-hour training exercise, at the most. "I've got my radio. I'll call the Coast Guard. Don't sweat it." He positioned himself behind the helm and turned on the engine. "I'll be fine. See you soon." He saluted and backed the yacht out of its slip.

Tonight's excursion would be good training for two reasons: not just operating the Majestic during the storm, but also during the darkness of night. Both could become challenges during the race, and although, as an experienced sailor, he'd managed them before, it never hurt to sharpen his skills.

He left the sails secured and motored through the marsh to where it opened into the Atlantic Ocean. It was immediately evident when he crossed over into open sea. Much stronger waves began spitting around him. The boat rocked, and he was surprised to lose his footing. He grabbed for something to hold on to, scrambling to get his feet solidly underneath him. Finally balanced, he moved across the deck, positioning himself in the center so he could raise the mainsail and the jib.

Another wave hit, and he grabbed hold of the empty mast. "Whoa, baby," he said aloud. Then, because the blowing wind was so loud, he repeated it, yelling, "Whoa, baby!" The storm was only just hitting this area, and it was already knocking him off his feet. He had two choices: turn around and go home, secure the yacht firmly in its slip and evacuate the storm. Or, continue with his plan to sail in it, heightening his skills and experiences for storm sailing.

As he released the main halyard and reached for the winch to raise the mainsail, it occurred to him that most sane people would've picked Option A. But they weren't competing in the Newport Bermuda race in two weeks, and those people didn't have the pressure of a major contract with Sailtone riding on a strong finish in the race. Those people didn't have the spirit of an extreme sport athlete.

He released the ties on the sails and checked them quickly to make sure they were ready to be extended. They all looked fine. Starting with the mainsail, he gripped the winch and pushed the crank around and around in a circle. He leaned back, watching the huge sail unfurl and travel up the mast. Halfway up, he stopped and examined the big sail from his vantage point on the deck. It flapped furiously in the mounting wind and Jett worried for a second that he wouldn't have the strength to continue to raise the sails manually, fighting the force of the storm gales. He took a moment to shake his arms out, softening the cramps in his biceps, then went back to it.

He proceeded to crank again, and the sail advanced higher and higher up the mast. When it was almost all the way up, it stopped. Jett leaned back and looked straight up, fifty feet in the air to see what was preventing the sail from reaching the top. He moved carefully to the port side, so he wasn't directly under the sail. Getting a better vantage point, and gripping onto the side of the boat, he looked up. There was some sort of obstruction. The sail wasn't completely raised.

Darkness had descended, and he was far from land now. He turned and made his way carefully below deck. He flipped on the deck lights, bathing the yacht in a glow. He grabbed his big flashlight and climbed back outside. He could see it now. The main halyard, or the line that connects to the sail, was tangled. The wind had whipped it around the mast, and as a result, it had not gone smoothly up.

He considered his options. He could sail without fixing the tangle. He wouldn't achieve optimum speed, but performance wasn't his priority tonight. Besides, when he raised the jib, he would get better wind distribution across both sails. He could just leave it and fix it when he lowered the sail at the end of his jaunt.

He made his way to the winch for the jib, and cranked it in a circle, while he watched the jib elevation carefully. The tangle had probably occurred when he'd stopped raising the mainsail halfway through. Learning from his own mistakes, he didn't pause this time. He raised the entire secondary sail and it went all the way to the top of the mast without issue.

Now, it was time to simply sail. Jett positioned himself in the center of the cockpit, so he could react to high waves and tossing by holding on. He cut the motor and decided to sail for twenty minutes, then reverse direction and sail back. The wind grabbed hold of the sails and drove the boat strongly out to sea. The waves were choppy, but the hull skimmed across without taking on water.

Fifteen minutes into the voyage, Jett noticed a calming in the sea. Had he outrun the storm? Was it chasing him, and would it reach him here soon? Or had the tropical storm changed directions and gone either north or south of him? Was this the worst the storm was going to hand him?

He released his grip and sampled keeping his balance without aid. Sure enough, he no longer needed to hold on for balance. The deck was horizontal and solid, and the waves were no longer throwing him around.

He shrugged. Mother Nature at its finest. As a sailor, you never knew what you were up against, and you certainly couldn't control the weather. You could just take what was handed to you and deal with it.

Time to head back. He grabbed the helm and started steering the boat to return to the dock. Now that the wind had died down, his attention was drawn back to the tangle at the top of the mainsail. He could probably fix it now. What was stopping him? Conditions were only slightly crazier than a normal day sail off the coast. Why wait?

A few years ago, Jett had installed metal footholds up the center of the mast, a ladder of sorts, so he could climb and perch high above the ship, watching the horizon. He'd wanted to do it because it reminded him of how a pirate would captain his ship. He'd often climbed up there while anchored out at sea, entertaining friends on the boat. Occasionally he used one of the metal steps as a high diving board, tossing himself away from the boat's surface and into the water.

He gazed up the mast's length and realized that without the strong tropical storm winds, he could safely climb up footholds to the top of the mast and untangle the halyard for the trip home. But first, better safe than sorry. He located a lifejacket in the cabin, then also grabbed a tether so he could connect himself safely to the mast as he climbed. He hopped onto the first step and stretched his legs to the second. He slowly climbed, carefully assessing the winds as he went. He wouldn't want to be up fifty feet in the air when the winds returned. But so far, everything was fine, and he reached the top without incident. He snapped the tether onto the closest step, then leaned his body away from the mast. Holding on with one hand, he reached his other arm out and grabbed the halyard. He tugged and came to a realization: after twenty minutes of sailing with the tangle, it was an unmerciful mess.

Leaning out as far as was safe, he tugged and pulled and made a tiny bit of progress and concluded that it wasn't worth it. He had little chance of untangling this mess now. He'd return home, lower the sails, and untangle the ropes on dry land.

Suddenly, the ship pitched violently. He not only lost his hand's hold on the mast, his feet scrambled off the footholds. Without a securing grip with his hands, his body dangled high in the air over the boat and the dark, angry sea, secured only by the harness tether. Far from dangling motionless, the strong tide caused his body to swing wildly back and forth. Heart racing, Jett scrambled to right himself. Reaching for the mast as he swung by, he missed it and had to wait for the next rotation. The ship angled heavily to the port side, and as he swung by, the mast was just out of reach of his fingers.

As he hung high in the air, the yacht straightened, and Jett recognized his opportunity. He grabbed the mast, pulled himself against it and held on with both hands, his feet coming to rest on a lower foothold. Hugging himself tight to the mast, he closed his eyes. Pulling a calming breath into his lungs, he clutched till his hands stopped shaking. He knew that motion was amplified here, at the top of the mast. Small movement below on the deck was huge at the top of the mast. Time to make his way down and go home.

Another rogue wave shook the boat wildly. He managed to hold on until a third wave caused the ship to pitch again. Airborne, the boat crashed hard back into the water. His left foot slid off the slippery metal ladder rung. He was now holding on with one hand and one foot. The next jolt did him in.

He swung away from the mast in open air, the harness preventing him from a terrifying freefall. On the return, the massive force crashed his body into a metal foothold. A cracking sound filled his ears. An intense ache ripped a scream from his lungs. He'd broken ribs, he was sure of it.

He grabbed hold of the ladder rung and kicked his free foot beneath him, blindly searching for another rung. The ship dipped deeply.

Because he had lit the ship up, he could see his descent. One agonizing descending step after another, his injury causing excruciating pain with every movement. A frantic plea for help flashed through his brain. *Help me, Lord.*

He reached the cockpit floor and lowered himself onto the deck, lying silently, taking stock of his body. With each pant of his breath, his ribs protested with pain, so he frantically tried to slow his breathing. Having difficulty calming himself as the ship pitched and rolled in the storm surge, he moved on to assess additional injuries. He methodically moved his hands and fingers. They were fine, all of them. He reached up and gently massaged his scalp and face. He felt a sore spot, which would certainly result in a big lump, and possibly a concussion. But no lacerations, no blood. That was a good thing.

His right knee was tender and swollen, which made full movement of it tricky. But when he slowly applied his body's weight on the leg, it held. It wasn't broken.

What to do? What to do? The worst of his injuries were the broken ribs, and each time he breathed too heavily, turned his torso or brushed against something, it caused an excruciating throb. He needed medical care, that was certain. Did he also need help getting his ship back to the dock?

Amidst the howling wind and the salty waves now splashing over the side of his ship and covering the floor, he made his decision. He'd get the boat back to dock, but he'd need help strapping it down, and then he'd get medical care at the hospital.

His dad's mantra, oft repeated throughout his entire childhood, played through his mind, *Suffer in silence, Jett.* He resisted the urge to shout out. It wouldn't do any good anyway.

Panting with pain and effort, he trudged below deck and activated the radio, relieved when he got a signal. Jett lifted the mouthpiece and said, "Mayday. Mayday. This is The Majestic and I need help."

Chapter Six

Sunday mornings were for church, regardless of what had gone on Saturday night, or was planned for later in the day. Sadie's dad had raised her that way, and now that she was old enough to make her own decisions, she continued with this habit.

She finished her preparations to her hair and makeup and swung downstairs to the kitchen. Dad sat at the table, drinking a cup of coffee and paging through the newspaper. Her lips formed into a fond smile. She loved that her dad still read an actual paper newspaper. He even folded it in fourths, so he could maneuver it better while eating his breakfast.

"Hi, Dad." As she walked past him he held out a hand and she gave it a slap. A daily high five was their standard greeting, followed by an occasional hug.

"Hi, Sadie girl." He looked up from the paper. "Mind driving yourself to church this morning? I'm swinging by to pick up Nora."

She looked over at him while she poured her cereal and milk. This was different. She and her dad had always ridden to church together, and over the last six months or so, Nora had met them there, and they'd all sit together in the pew. In the fifth pew back on the right side of the sanctuary, in fact. As far over on the aisle side as possible.

"Okay," she said, drawing it out like it was a question. If Dad caught the intent, he didn't comment.

"Whoever's there first, save seats for the others." He got up, tossed his remaining coffee down the drain and placed the cup in the sink. He strode across the kitchen and out the door without another word.

She frowned and moved to the window to watch him get into his truck. Wait, was that a whistle she heard? Her dad was whistling a happy tune? She shrugged, grabbed her bowl of cereal and sat at the table to eat.

Later, she arrived at Oceanview Church. Nora and her dad sat in their normal spot, so she made her way over, admiring, as she always did, the clear plate-glass window behind the altar. Everyone who sat in the sanctuary facing the preacher had the gift of staring out at the beautiful inlet. Sand, water, piers and wildlife, along with the sun sparkling off the water. Those ambitious enough to get themselves out of bed for the sunrise service received a special treat. The church was situated on prime beachfront real estate, a long-term treasure established before costs had skyrocketed. For someone like herself, who always found inspiration in a beach setting, it was the perfect church to attend.

Sadie slid into her seat. "Good morning, Nora." She nodded at her dad's girlfriend with a smile. She sat furthest away from Sadie, with Dad between them.

"Good morning," Nora murmured.

"Sadie, we have something to tell you."

A weight fell on Sadie's chest. It always did when someone said something like, "We have something to tell you." Whether that something turned out to be good or bad, she couldn't help her body's natural reaction. "What?" she asked breathlessly.

Her dad and Nora smiled at each other, and then Nora put her hand in Dad's. He pulled it gently in Sadie's direction. And that's when Sadie saw it. Nora wore a solid gold band encrusted with rows of diamonds. It had never been there before, so what else could a ring like that mean? Especially since Dad and Nora appeared so happy.

"You got married?" she exclaimed, much louder than she intended. Because now their neighboring pew mates heard her.

"Congratulations!"

"Congratulations, you two."

"So happy for you."

Sadie couldn't decide if she was happy for them, because she was fond of Nora and knew she made a great match for her dad, or upset that they hadn't informed her of their pending marriage before they went ahead and did the deed. What was that called, an elopement? Sadie guessed she couldn't blame them for eloping, but wow, she sure would've liked to have been at the wedding.

The buzzing surrounding Dad and Nora went on for a little while until Dad stood up and slashed his hand in the air, putting an end to it. "Now, just hold on there," he ordered, whether to Sadie, or to everyone in the church who was commenting. "We didn't get married. Yet. We got engaged."

Nora came to her feet, holding on to Shaw's arm. A flush of regret ran through Sadie. Nora and her dad were both embarrassed by the unwelcome attention, and, well, it was all her fault.

"That's not a wedding ring?"

Her dad shook his head at her. "No."

"You didn't elope?"

"No."

Sadie stood and pulled them both into an embrace. "I'm so happy for you! Congratulations. You have my blessing to go ahead and get married."

Her dad laughed, thank goodness, and so did Nora. They were handling it with good cheer. "I'm sorry I messed that up," she whispered to her dad, but he shook his head. He didn't care. They were among their church family, everyone was happy for them, and her dad was the happiest she'd ever seen him.

Sadie released them, and all the neighboring church members re-congratulated them, for their engagement this time. Meanwhile, Pastor Ralph had taken the pulpit and he gazed curiously over at the disturbance. "Does someone have an announcement to make before we begin worship?"

Her dad looked up and a faint blush colored his neck. He gripped Nora's hand tighter and replied in a public speaking voice, "Nora and I are engaged to be married."

The pastor broke out into a happy smile. "Congratulations to you both. We wish you all the best. In fact, could you both join me in the reception hall after the service to shake hands with the congregation? I'm sure they'll all want to express their well wishes in person."

They all sat, and the service began. Sadie glanced over at Nora and her dad, eyebrows up. She felt responsible for the invitation from the pastor, and she hoped they both felt comfortable about it. But they looked fine, and her dad, at least, had been a member here his entire adult life and knew everyone. One of the great things about being a part of a church community. People who loved you, who grieved your losses and celebrated your blessings.

Sadie concentrated on the worship service, but excitement shivered through her. She sure hoped Nora would let her help plan their wedding.

~ * ~

Performing his job duties as a physical trainer without being able to twist his torso or increase his rate of breathing was not easy. Jett was also restricted on the amount of weight he could lift. But it was possible. After missing three days of work after his sailing accident, he finally convinced his boss at the gym that he could be effective as a trainer for his clients, just not quite as hands-on as he was before his injury.

On his first day back, Jett worked with Joe who was in his early fifties, facing his empty nest years, and woefully out of shape from decades of sitting: working at a desk all day and watching his kids' sporting activities almost every night. Now, his kids were independent, and it was time for him to get his body primed for a new active lifestyle. Jett had developed a workout plan that included everything in moderation. Cardio in the form of brisk walking, light jogging and bicycling, and weight training three times a week involving light, long sets on the weight machine.

"Looking good," Jett said as he watched Joe perform three sets of ten on his bicep weight. At Joe's age, the worst mistake he could make was to jump into an advanced exercise program that was much too demanding for a body that hadn't been active in so long. A slow, steady start was the best approach for avoiding injury, and Joe was doing great.

Joe finished his last rep and stood, grabbing his nearby towel and swiping it over his forehead. "Thanks. I'll ride twenty miles on the bike tomorrow and see you back here on Wednesday for more weight training." He pointed a sympathetic glance at Jett's side. "Sorry about your boating accident. Fractured ribs are no fun."

Jett sighed. "Yeah, but it could've been a lot worse." He waved Joe off to the showers and he returned to the front desk to glance at his calendar. He had a two-hour break between clients. Which was good because he had a more important job to do.

He'd already made a half dozen phone calls. He'd started with calls to friends who were expert sailors. Receiving rejections, he moved to casual sailors, before moving on to his last choice of friends who had at least ridden on Jett's boat once before. He'd even approached his slipmate at the marina, Mark. He offered the opportunity of a lifetime, a chance to accompany him on the Newport Bermuda race and aid him where his own physical abilities fell short. With the fracture injury being so fresh, he wouldn't be 100% when it came to maneuvering around the boat, climbing up the mast ladder, down to the cabin. He needed a first mate. He would still do the majority of the sailing, but when he needed help, he would give the orders and his mate would carry them out.

What a chance-of-a-lifetime he was offering to someone! A chance he personally would jump on if he were in their shoes.

Why was it then, that every single one of those he contacted turned him down flat? What was wrong with his delivery that they didn't see the phenomenal opportunity he was offering them?

He pulled a written list out of his shorts pocket. Each name had been crossed off, only one remained. It was a long-shot, and even as he'd written the name, Sam, down, he never thought he'd get to the bottom of the list. He never dreamed that he'd have a half dozen rejections.

He pulled out his cell phone and accessed a long-dormant number in his Contacts. Placing the call, he was glad that it still worked. A few rings later, Sam's voice responded, "Hello."

"Hi Sam." Jett kept his voice light and positive. Showing his desperation for a 'yes' was not the way to go here. "I'm giving you a blast from your past here."

"Who is this?"

"Jett Martin."

"Jett?"

"Yes, hi. It's been at least, what, eight years?"

"Wow. Yeah! How are you, Jett?"

"Doing great. I hope you don't mind a call out of the blue."

"Nah, I've got a few minutes. Still sailing?"

Jett's heart warmed at the question. Sam had been Jett's first sailing instructor, other than Jett's dad. Once Jett had determined he needed to break free from his father's watchful eye and move out into competitive sailing on his own, he'd researched and found Sam. "Yeah, sure am. It's a big part of my life now. You sure put me on firm footing to pursue a career of competitive yacht sailing."

"Yeah, yeah, now that you mention it, I saw your name on the gold medal list for a race I competed in last month. The Clipper Open Yacht Race."

Jett smiled. "Yes! I placed gold in that one about two years ago, I think."

"Awesome job, man." They chatted easily about some of the races they'd competed in, the brotherhood of racing binding them together.

"I have a favor to ask you," Jett said. "Or an opportunity for you, depending on how you look at it."

"Tell me."

"I'm enrolled in the Newport Bermuda race in two weeks, in the single-handed division. But I've banged up my ribs and I won't be able to do it all myself. I'm looking for a partner to sail with me in the double-handed division. Someone experienced who can jump in without a ton of practice. I need to finish strong in this race. Without going into a lot of detail, I've got a contract riding on this finish. This injury couldn't have come at a worse time."

"Newport Bermuda. That's a cool race, man. Never done it."

Sam's interest caused Jett's pulse to race. Maybe this would be a yes. "It goes from Newport, Rhode Island to Bermuda over open seas. Plan on spending about four or five days at sea. You'd be a great partner, man, my first choice. And what a great race for your resume. I knew it had been a while since we'd been in contact, but I had to reach out to you. What do you say?"

A silent pause caused Jett's pulse to pound in his ears.

"When is it?"

"Weekend after next." Jett gave him the dates.

"Aww, dude." His words and his tone made Jett's optimism crash. "I've been promising a vacation to my wife and kids for almost a year. We'll be on an airplane that day. Sorry, Jett."

Disappointment flooded his senses. His final prospect, gone. What was he going to do? His mind whirring, he tried to continue a friendly conversation with his old coach and end the call with a promise to get together soon. But when he sat in the silence of the final rejection, he had no idea what to do. If it were just the race, he'd withdraw his spot. But there was a great deal riding on his not only competing but winning the race: the Sailtone contract.

For years, his little invention had been just an idea he'd had, based on the frequency with which sails were damaged due to the sun. At first, he started experimenting with sunscreen chemicals to help his own sails last longer. Allow him to save money on replacing sails and spend it on something else. But when Sailtone advertised the showcase for new inventions in the world of sailing, it seemed like a message from God: *do this.* It was against his character. He never thought of himself as a full-blown adult with brains and ambition. In fact, no one did. His friends didn't. His parents didn't. The persona he put out to the world was much different. Fun, easygoing, athletic, not a care in the world. A happy-go-lucky kid who loved sailing and the boats and the ocean, making ends meet with his trainer job while pursuing his dream.

But when he'd put together his pitch and made it through the showcase to the next step, he started thinking, maybe that could change. If Sailtone offered him a contract for this product, and if it were useful in the world of sailing, his whole life would change. He'd have a steady stream of income from his invention, which would allow him to cut loose from the trainer job. It would allow him to stretch his dream to the fullest, which was sailing around the world. Map out a course where he would stop at ports along the way and thoroughly absorb the culture. See places he'd never dreamed of seeing. Maybe take a camera along with him and film himself on the high seas, and in the ports, interacting with the people. Would a movie producer be interested in that footage for a documentary?

It was possible.

He was dreaming big, he realized that. But it would never happen without this first step. Compete in the race, place in the top three and get the contract from Sailtone to take his invention into manufacturing. The offer was fleeting, they'd made that clear. If he passed this race up due to his broken ribs, it could be a missed opportunity for the rest of his life. And how depressing would that be?

He focused his mind on ... who. Who else could he call and invite to join him? His thoughts transformed into a silent prayer, *Lord, help me find someone who wants to help me. Help me out of this problem I'm in. Help me.*

The door opened. He looked up and saw Sadie Flynn.

~ * ~

Sadie strode through the front door of the gym, ready to sneak in forty minutes of cardio before returning to school for her next class. She walked by the front desk and saw a familiar face. "Hi, Jett." She would've continued her trek to the gym equipment except for two things.

The beaming smile on Jett's face at the sight of her. And his pleased exclamation, "Sadie!"

She came to a fast halt. "Hello there." She frowned, curious at his reaction. Sure, he was always pleasant. But not this ... ecstatic at the sight of her.

He came around the desk. "Hey, do you have a minute? Or two? Or even more?"

She shook her head. "No, I don't. I'm in between classes and wanted to get in a workout."

He nodded vigorously. "Where are you going? I'll go with you. There's something I want to talk to you about."

She considered, then pointed to the treadmill. "Maybe just jog for forty minutes or so."

"Great."

They made their way over to the treadmill. Sadie placed her water bottle in the cup holder and started her stretches. "So, what's up?"

"I need to talk to you about something," Jett said.

"Right. What is it?" She continued through her normal full-body stretches that preceded all her workouts and turned her head to gaze at Jett. For some reason he was hemming and hawing, hesitant to tell her. A dreadful thought popped into her head. He wasn't going to ask her out again, was he? She was still undecided whether the first time he'd asked, it was a dinner invitation between two friends or an actual date. But if he asked her again ... she'd definitely have to set him straight. "Out with it."

He gave a determined nod. "Okay. I need some help. And you're the perfect person to do it."

She finished stretching and mounted the treadmill. Pushing buttons on the control panel, she started at a walking pace. "Sure. What is it?"

"Did I tell you about the race I have coming up?"

"A sailboat race? No, not that I remember."

"I'm enrolled in a prestigious race called the Newport Bermuda. The course is Newport, Rhode Island to the island of Bermuda. It'll take four or five days. I enrolled because it's the first time this race has opened up single-handed sailing. But I broke a few ribs and I can't carry out all the responsibilities needed for that type of sail."

"What happened?"

He shrugged. "I was doing a training exercise and got injured." He patted his side gently. "Two broken ribs. Hurts like the dickens every time I twist, lift or try to run. Wouldn't be safe for me to sail without help."

She nodded. "What a shame! So, you have to drop out?"

He shook his head vigorously. "No. I can't drop out. Well, I don't want to. Even though it's not my normal category, I'd switch my enrollment to the double-handed division."

Her warmup done, Sadie pushed into a jog. "You're looking for a first mate."

"Yes," he said, and she couldn't ignore the delighted smile that decorated his face. The guy had good looks, she couldn't deny that.

"Someone to go on this race with you?"

"Yes, exactly."

"What does this have to do with me?"

"Well," he stammered, looked down at his feet and back up at her, "I want you to be my first mate."

She turned to stare directly into his eyes and her jogging came to a halt. She rode the treadmill backwards and it deposited her onto the floor. "What?"

He walked to her side and touched her arm. "Are you okay?"

"Yes, but ... what?"

"You would be a great first mate. You're strong and athletic and you love a physical challenge."

"True. Those would all be reasons to take me on a boat ride. Not compete in a top-level yachting race as first mate! I have no idea what I'm doing, Jett."

"But I do! All you'd have to do is listen to me and do what I say."

She frowned.

He grinned. "You listened to me and did what I said when you were training for your first marathon, right? And look how well that turned out."

"This is crazy! I've been on a sailboat once in my entire life! This is a big-time race you're enrolled in. I'm not qualified to race a yacht. Think about this. A double-handed race team means both sailors are at the top of their skillset. Not one expert and one novice."

He squeezed her arm and a small jolt of electricity passed through their contact. "I know, believe me. But I wouldn't ask you if I didn't think you could do it."

Sadie paused, thinking. She stepped back onto the treadmill and resumed her jogging. She shook her head as her heartrate rose. "This is crazy. I have no skills to help you. And no time to develop them. In fact, you said four or five days, right? There's no way I could leave class that long."

"I know there's a time commitment. I know it's a lot to ask. But believe me when I tell you that I'm in a bind. I don't usually have to ask for help and I'm not comfortable with it. I wouldn't ask you if it weren't really important."

She glanced at him. She knew his words were true. Jett was always a solo act. He managed his own personal trainer clients, and he was a single-handed captain in racing competitions. He relied on no one. He was completely self-sufficient. Except now. He'd injured himself and couldn't do it alone. She knew how hard it was for him to ask. Still, she couldn't spare the time. "Surely you have better options to help you than me. Don't you know any expert sailors like yourself who would like to do this?"

He dropped his head. "I do, and I've already asked them. Most of my sailing friends have jobs and families and can't take off with such short notice."

She laughed. "So, I'm your last resort?"

"No! I didn't mean it that way."

She gazed at him, her silence full of meaning.

"Well, okay, you weren't the first person I thought of. But that doesn't mean you wouldn't be awesome at it. Please, Sadie. Do you want me to beg? Because I'm not above begging." He lowered himself to a kneel and gripped his hands together, pointing them in her direction. "Ple-e-e-ase, Sadie. Please help me. I'll do whatever you want. I'll pay you ... if I can put it on a periodic payment plan. Or, better yet, I'll give you free trainer services."

Sadie hopped off the treadmill and grabbed his arms, pulling him to a standing position. "Stop! Stop begging. I don't want your money and I don't need your trainer services anymore." She smiled at him, her head whirring. "Honestly, I don't know why you don't just cancel.

Maybe it's not meant to be. Wait till your ribs heal and sign up for another race."

He let out a breath and looked into her eyes. "I have a lot riding on this race. For my future. I have a unique opportunity and it all hinges on doing well in this particular race. If I have to wait until my ribs heal, it may be gone."

Sadie frowned as she studied his face. Gone was the happy-go-lucky Jett she'd always known, without a care in the world. This was a serious Jett, with stakes on the line. "What is it?"

"I'll show you. Have a minute?" He gestured toward the front desk, walked over there, and Sadie followed him. He reached under the counter, pulled out a small jar and twisted the lid. He pulled out a foot-square piece of fabric.

He looked up at her. "I have a patented invention. A company called Sailtone is interested in it. Their Research and Development department wants to get it into the cycle, and I had a meeting with them recently. We now have a signed contract saying that if I place in the top three of the Newport Bermuda race, they'll designate funding into developing it for retail."

Sadie stared, first at Jett, then at the items he'd pulled out. She could hardly believe what he was telling her. Jett had invented something that could be important to the sailing world? Although she wasn't surprised he had the brains or knowledge to do it, she wouldn't have guessed he had the discipline. There was so much more to Jett under the surface than she'd always assumed. Nice guy, physically fit, wanted to help others. But this? This was a revelation.

"Wow, I don't know what to say. What is your invention all about?"

Jett gave her a brief explanation about the damage that the sun's UV rays inflict on sails under long-term exposure. He explained his product was like a sunscreen for the fabric, and it pretty much removed the exposure damage. He'd been using it himself for two years with amazing results on his own sails. And he had this big-time boating company interested in it. It all came down to this race.

This race that he had to place in the top three to secure the contract.

This race that he now faced with broken ribs fresh from injury, restricting his movement. He needed a helper so he wouldn't face further injury, maneuvering around the boat.

"This race is important for me, personally, because of the Sailtone contract. But also, I just really love sailing. The beauty of the water, the unpredictability of the waves, the chance to master the sea. There's nothing like it. It dangerous, yes. But I'm still addicted to trying to succeed over whatever nature throws me. It's a kick, it really is." He smiled. "And I predict that if you give yourself a chance, you'll grow to love it as much as I do."

His passion was evident. On its surface, the opportunity seemed custom-made for her. Hadn't she just been researching her next extreme sporting adventure? Hadn't she identified a gap in her life that could only be filled with an intense physical challenge? Something she'd never tried before? And then this fell into her lap.

But it seemed unlikely that she could be of any help. She had no experience with boats; she had no idea what she was doing. Not to mention, he was asking her to miss at least a week of classes, maybe more. And what about chance of injury? If Jett had broken ribs, and he was an expert, what if she had an accident while on the race? She'd be setting herself up for more delay in her education. She'd already paid for this semester of classes. If she missed time due to the race and potential recovery, would she have to drop out?

He finished his impromptu demonstration and she pushed her frustration out in a whoosh. "Oh Jett. I don't know. I am so impressed with this." She gestured. "With you. I had no idea you were working on a product like this. That is super cool." She looked into his eyes and gave him a tentative smile, hoping he knew how sincere she was. "And I'd love to help you achieve your dreams. Just like you helped me achieve mine." Her mind raced to the program he'd put her on a few years ago to prepare her for that first marathon. She couldn't have done it without him. "But, wow. It's a lot to ask. Seriously. I'm a college student and I can't just leave for a week or more. I'd get so behind in school that it could drag down my grades."

He nodded gravely. "Yeah, I understand." He slowly screwed the lid back on the jar and folded up the sail sample. "It is a lot to ask. Can I just ask you one more thing? Think about it. Please? Over the next twenty-four hours, give it some thought and let me know tomorrow." He gripped her hands in both of his and squeezed gently. "Either way, whether you can do it or not, I appreciate you giving it some consideration."

She looked into his eyes, sadder than she'd ever seen them, and her heart broke. Surely it couldn't just be down to her. Surely, he had better options. Someone better suited, someone better qualified. And yet, he said he'd asked others and they'd turned him down. For a brief second, she almost said yes, just to restore the characteristic happiness to his eyes, to his face, to his smile. But she restrained herself.

"I'll do that, Jett. I will give it some thought to see if I can possibly get away from school that long without sabotaging my entire semester."

He nodded his thanks.

Chapter Seven

After class that afternoon, Sadie had a private discussion with her professor and offered the possibility that she would miss a week of class. They looked over his schedule together.

Her professor shook his head. "We have a test less than a week after you return. It would be difficult to prepare yourself. And that test is worth 25% of your semester grade, so it holds a lot of weight."

She nodded while her heart took a disappointed flip. "Thanks."

He closed his coursebook. "Think long and hard before you leave. It may have devastating results on your class grade. Summer sessions are already condensed as it is."

Studying later that evening, she stretched her arms above her head to work out the kinks in her spine. She pulled up the internet browser and typed in the name of the race Jett was talking about, Newport Bermuda. The race's website popped up. Photos of beautiful yachts and videos of competitors racing across the sea consumed her for fifteen minutes. Then she typed in the name of the company interested in Jett's sunscreen lotion for sails. It, as well, had a large professional website. Although she'd never heard of Sailtone, it was evidently a big deal in the boating industry.

Imagine Jett, her carefree trainer here in Murrells Inlet, playing in the big time of the sailing industry. He had so much going for him, and yet, never bragged about his accomplishments. She'd worked with him on almost a daily basis for months and he'd never talked about this great passion of his. And yet, today when he'd talked about yacht racing his excitement was contagious. He'd captured her interest and her desire not only to help him, but to experience this extreme sport herself. If only she had the free time.

She stood and stretched her legs on a short walk around the house. She'd thought of a bunch of reasons why this wouldn't work. Now what if she focused on how to get beyond those obstacles so she could help her friend with his goals, experience a new extreme sport of her own, while not destroying her semester's grades? Surely this wasn't an insurmountable problem. Could she get the class assignments ahead of time? Work on them before she left? Set up a make-up session with her professor when she returned to make sure she was prepared for the test? Ask for a week's delay for the test if needed?

She wasn't one to back down from a challenge. Her nature required her to face it head on and succeed.

She took one last look at the race website as an excited smile burst onto her face. This felt right, for so many reasons. She reached for her phone and called Jett. When she said her name, she felt his gasp, more than heard it. "I'll do it."

"Wait, are you sure?"

"Yes. I'll be your first mate on the race."

She heard a whoop of joy through the phone, but it was distant, muted. "Jett?" she asked, laughing. "Are you there?"

"Yeah, sorry, I threw my phone up in the air."

She laughed. "I have some obstacles to overcome at school, and of course, you need to train me on what you want me to do, but I'm in. I'm committed."

A moment of silence, then, Jett's sincere voice, "Thank you. I can't thank you enough for helping me. Together, we just might make my dreams come true."

"Well, I can't promise you we'll win. In fact, we'll be coming in as underdogs. Our team of two only has one real sailor. The other teams have two."

"It's okay. Without you, I was left on the shore. With you, I'm back in the game."

They made plans for their first training session and Sadie hung up. Her heart raced with the reality of what she'd just agreed to do. She wouldn't sleep well tonight. A combination of excitement and anxiety would play with her head. But the adrenaline racing through her veins was a feeling she was familiar with. Great things started with this feeling.

~ * ~

Dressed in a one-piece swimsuit, covered with gym shorts and a nylon tank top, Sadie drove to the Wicked Sisters Marina. She'd slipped on a pair of running shoes, hoping that it would help her maneuver around the boat surfaces, and she slathered on a thick layer of sunscreen. As far as she knew, she was ready for her sailing lesson.

She parked and made her way to the boat slip. Jett was already there, inside the boat cabin, his curly longish brown hair popping in and out. When he spotted her, he raised his hand in a wave. It was his happy, carefree smile that caught and held her attention. Knowing that she had put that smile there made her happy.

"Hi," she greeted him. He bobbed up and down gently in the boat while she stood on the taller pier, looking down at him.

"Hey there." He crossed the cabin and held out a hand to her. "Ready to go out?"

"Absolutely." She took his hand and boarded the boat.

He surprised her by pulling her in for a hug. He murmured in her ear, "I know I thanked you last night on the phone, but I can't thank you enough for doing this."

A shiver ran through her shoulders at his closeness. She shook it off. Pulling in a steadying breath, she wondered briefly what scent adorned his skin. It came as a surprise to her that he'd sprayed on some cologne for their lesson. She wouldn't have guessed him to be a guy who bothered. "You're welcome." She pulled back to look into his eyes. "I think you have an amazing opportunity with Sailtone, and I don't want you to miss out on that. If I can help keep you in the game, I'm happy to do it. In addition, I had been thinking about my next extreme sport opportunity. Let's just say you saved me from jumping out of a plane."

He chuckled. "Over a hundred hours in a sailboat traveling down the coast of the eastern United States, versus, what, a couple of minutes plummeting to earth from an airplane."

She grinned. "Yeah, which one's crazier?" She glanced around the ship interior. "What's first, coach?"

He bent at the waist and picked up a lifejacket that was lying on the floor. "This. We'll both wear lifejackets for all training and the actual race."

She shrugged, nodded and put it on. "Okay, safety first. Next?"

His gaze rested on her for a moment. "We'll go through everything in chronological order. I'll do it first while you watch, then you do it too. The first thing we do is release the boat from the dock. Then, we maneuver out of the slip, into the marsh channel, then into open sea."

An excited shudder went through her. "Cool."

He made his way to the side of the yacht, then hopped out onto the pier. He grimaced at the motion and brought a hand up to his torso.

"How's your injury?"

He looked at her and rolled his eyes. "I mean, broken ribs are touchy when you move certain ways. One minute it's fine, but if I twist or turn the wrong way, it reminds me with pain. I'm used to flying around this ship, around the deck, up the mast, down into the cabin, no problem. Now, I have to slow down and be careful."

Standing on the wooden pier, he faced the boat. "Our first lesson is about how the boat is secured to the dock. You notice it's tied with three lines." He walked to the front. "The front of the boat is called the bow. So this one," he pointed to the line running from the bow of the ship to a metal hitch screwed to the dock, "is the bow line." He walked the length of the yacht and pointed. "The back of the boat is called the stern. So this one is called …."

"The stern line?" she asked.

"You got it. The third one is the spring and helps keep it centered on the pier. I rarely use more than three." He untied the line at the stern and coiled it neatly, while her mind repeated, *the front is the bow, the back is the stern.* That seemed important.

"Want to get the bow line undone while I'm doing this one?"

She nodded and went to work, then when they had two neatly coiled lines, they boarded the boat again and released the middle line.

"Next, we use the engine to get underway."

She was so out of her element. Until she'd sailed with him, she hadn't really thought about sailboats having engines. Now that she thought about it, it made sense that they did. They wouldn't be able to rely on the wind to get in and out of the harbor.

They moved to the steering wheel and she watched him as he turned on the engine, explaining as he went. He slowly moved the boat out of the slip, using a combination of backing up, inching forward and rudder shifts until finally they were able to safely leave the pier behind. "You ready to take the helm, Skipper?"

"Now?"

He nodded. "Sure. We're just going through open waters towards the sea, then we'll put the sails up and capture the wind."

She put her hand on the wheel and tried not to think about the expensive vessel that was now under her control. Of course, Jett was right beside her, so before she did anything crazy like run it aground, he would prevent her.

"Remember what that wheel feels like?" he said.

"Sure do, and this time I won't jerk it too fast," she said. It really wasn't too different from driving a car, except of course, the vehicle was the size of a semi-truck and the road was water and had no lanes.

Eventually they made their way to the spot where the inlet waters met the Atlantic Ocean. She could tell because of the change in the color of the water, and the waves were much stronger. She glanced over at Jett and he nodded his approval, encouraging her to continue.

"Okay, now, the real fun starts. The wind is our motor for the majority of our time in this boat. I have two sails; the mainsail, which is the larger sail at midship; and the jib, which is the smaller sail toward the bow. To raise the sails, I use the winch to crank the halyards attached to each sail till the sails are tight."

Sadie studied him, his words sinking in. She nodded. "The words are unusual, but the concept doesn't seem too hard," she said hopefully.

"The biggest challenge is understanding the rigging, how the boat is set up, what each of these lines do, what sails they're attached to." He took a moment to walk her through each line, so she began to understand the purpose of each one. Now she just had to remember them. Her head started to swim. "Now we want to point the boat into the wind, to make it easier to hoist the sails."

He walked back to the helm. Looking around and holding up his hand, he determined the direction of the wind and used the wheel to maneuver the yacht into it. He pointed to the stern. "You release the sheets for the mainsail and I'll release the sheets for the jib."

She nodded, understanding the command, and did as he ordered. The lines needed to be loose enough so that when the sails were hoisted to full height, the lines didn't hold them back.

"All set," he said. He pointed to the winch with a big crank handle. "You're going use that to hoist the mainsail."

A flurry of excitement went through her as she made her way to the winch. She gripped the handle and glanced over at him.

"You're the muscle. I'll be the eyes to make sure everything goes smoothly. If I yell to stop, do it right away." He nodded at her, and she started cranking. And cranking, and cranking. The ratcheting sound of the winch filled her ears and she focused her gaze on the manual machinery, doing her best. Within minutes, her biceps ached with the effort of cranking the thing. She took a breather and stopped, pulling herself out of her concentration to glance up at the sail. Good Lord, it was only about a third of the way up! She had a ways to go.

"Keep going!" Jett yelled.

She shook out her arm and grabbed the crank handle again. More cranking. But eventually the sail puffed in the air, and she knew she was almost there.

"Okay, slow down."

She reduced her cranking speed and glanced straight up to see the beautiful white sail with blue stripes flipping and capturing the wind.

"Keep going. All looks good, you just have a little ways to go."

She cranked until he told her to stop, and then she collapsed onto a bench on the side of the cabin. "Wow! Talk about a bicep workout."

Jett hopped down to where she sat, and chuckled. "Sure is. And you're only halfway done."

"What?" Her eyes popped open wide.

"You still have the jib to do," he said, smiling. She massaged her aching bicep until he said, "I'm just kidding. Take the helm and steer into the wind while I'm raising the jib." She took her spot and tried to duplicate what she'd seen him do. When he used the winch crank she swore it only took him a fraction of the time she'd taken for the mainsail, and that was with an injury. She watched him work and a wave of admiration surged through her. She could understand the attraction to sailing. She'd never had the opportunity, but if she'd grown up this way, she'd never want to leave the boat.

Satisfied with the sails, he came over and cut the engine. "Nice sun today," he said. He lifted his face to the sun, then removed his lifejacket.

In a single movement, he pulled off the t-shirt he was wearing, exposing a broad, tanned and muscular torso. She stopped herself from gaping. She'd seen it before, of course. They'd sailed together and he'd trained her in the gym. But she had to recognize the sprinkle of physical attraction she felt for Jett, wearing his swim trunks, that beautiful bare chest and his biceps bulging as he worked with the boat. The man was a living picture of health and physical fitness.

She tore her eyes away. No. She would not allow herself to start developing feelings for him. They had a job to do. They both had a great deal at stake and they needed to focus on preparing her for the sailing race, then executing and finishing in the top three. He had a lot riding on a successful finish, and she needed to help him win, then get back to school.

Admiring his biceps and his abdominals and his gleaming tanned skin ... was the worst kind of distraction.

She wondered if she should ask him to put his shirt back on. No, that would be lame. That would let him know she was having trouble seeing him without it. And she didn't want to admit that.

So, she needed to stay focused on her work and get this race behind them.

"What's next?" she asked and stood.

He glanced at her and smiled. "Sailing."

"Let's have at it."

Chapter Eight

Jett and Sadie carved out a couple of hours every day for the next week to work on the basics of sailing. Although she was a total novice, Jett was pleased to see that Sadie caught on quickly and retained the knowledge she'd absorbed in previous days. He rarely had to repeat himself about concepts already learned. This didn't surprise him. He knew Sadie was smart, ambitious and athletic. Although sailing was new to her, she applied all the discipline and determination needed to learn it.

Most of sailing involved a few things: first, the vast vocabulary. The fathers of sailing had created a bunch of unique words that sailors needed to memorize, when they could have used normal words. Sadie was still struggling with some of them, but it didn't matter. Just the two of them would be on the boat so he could translate what she didn't remember. For example, the steering wheel was called the helm. Ropes were called sheets, or lines or halyards. The right side of the boat was the starboard and the left was the port.

The second thing they practiced over and over again was maximizing the strength of the wind. The tack, which was turning into the wind. And the jibe, turning with the wind coming from behind. These concepts were vital to sailing at optimum speed, which they would be doing in the race if they had a chance of placing high at the end. A long-term sailing race was a combination of taking advantage of sailing fast when the wind was good and killing time when the wind was bad. Sort of like a mathematical equation ... adding all the good and bad times together to present the best overall time.

The good thing was, he would make the decisions about making optimum use of the winds. She would be the muscles to shift the sails. With his brain and her brawn, they would form one perfect sailor.

Jett drove to Sadie's house at five am. Early morning darkness covered the small beach town and the crunching of his truck tires on the gravel seemed inordinately loud in the inactive silence. He parked and slowly pivoted his torso to lower himself to the ground. The soreness caused by the broken ribs was the bane of his existence, but he tried to count his blessings because he hadn't lost the privilege of competing in the race.

At Sadie's front door, he tapped quietly with one knuckle. She immediately opened it and the excited beaming smile on her face sent a rush of adrenaline down his esophagus to settle in his stomach. Along with it, his breath was swept away, so when he greeted her with, "Good morning," it was a whisper.

She didn't seem to notice as she said in a low voice, "Hey there. All ready?" She stepped aside and gestured him into the small living room of the bungalow.

"Yep."

She turned and took a few steps toward the back of the house, turning her head to say over her shoulder, "I don't think you've ever met my dad. Would you like to?"

"Of course." He followed her.

At the kitchen table sat a man dressed in jeans, a flannel shirt, and cowboy boots. A western hat sat on the counter near the back door. He looked like he could've been an actor for old westerns, with his slim build and handsome face. He seemed like the kind of man who made his living outdoors and was comfortable there, like he hadn't sat behind a desk or a computer screen a minute of his life. Jett could relate.

"Dad, this is Jett." Sadie made a gesture with her hand like she was presenting Jett to the king. "Jett, this is my dad, Shaw Flynn."

"Nice to meet you." Jett held out a hand for a shake. Sadie's dad got to his feet and took Jett's hand in a firm handshake. He towered over Jett by a good two inches. Head bent slightly, Shaw focused his full attention on Jett's eyes, as if he was searching for something there.

"Yeah, I've been wanting to meet you, too, Jett, ever since Sadie told me about this race you're doing together. I think I understand what you're doing, and why you asked Sadie to sail with you." Standing beside her father, Sadie rolled her eyes and gave Jett a tolerant smile. "But what I want to hear from you is, how dangerous is this race for a sailing novice like Sadie? Other than the sailing lessons you've given her for a week, she has no experience whatsoever. And as I understand it, this is a very competitive race."

Jett nodded and thought about his answer. "You're right. This is a top-level race. I've been working a long time to compete here. This dang injury put an end to that, for this year, at least. But Sadie may have told you I have a lot riding on not only competing but finishing well in this particular race."

"Yes, she's very impressed with your sunscreen invention for sails and believes it's a great product for sailors. I see what's in it for you, if Sadie helps you. But let's put that aside a moment. My question is, what's in it for Sadie?" He cleared his throat. "Why should she miss a week's school and jeopardize her semester grades in order to go do this with you and risk injury?"

Jett glanced down at his feet. *Well, Dad, if you put it like that ...* Jett understood fathers. He had a doozy of one himself. A father who had high expectations and never showed his approval for Jett's unconventional path in life. A father who'd wanted Jett to follow in his own footsteps into the military, an expectation he'd pounded into Jett his whole life. But that didn't stop Jett from pursuing his own path, to the disgust of his overbearing father.

He lifted his chin and looked at Sadie's dad. This man was different. He cared for his daughter. He knew Sadie was an adult and would make her own decisions, but that didn't stop him from asking questions to keep Sadie safe. To keep her from making mistakes she'd regret later.

"Sir, I understand your concern. At first glance, it may appear that I'm taking advantage of Sadie. That I'm asking her to put herself at risk for something that I want. It may seem unusual that she agreed to this plan." He glanced at Sadie, and she seemed intent on listening to his response to her father. He focused back on Shaw. "Sadie and I have worked together before, I don't know if she told you that. I was her physical trainer when she was working toward her first marathon. I witnessed first hand what a dedicated athlete she was, and I was impressed with her drive. Now, she's not only an accomplished multi-marathoner, she seeks out the thrill of extreme sports to feed her adrenaline."

Shaw nodded. "I'm aware."

"So, when Sadie agreed to accompany me on this race, yes, she solved my problem. But I also think she'll get a great deal out of it, too. She'll learn about yacht racing, first hand. She'll get to try something new, and she'll push her body to the limit. Not to mention the thrill of competition."

Shaw let that sit for a moment. "You're a highly experienced sailor and you injured yourself. Where does that put Sadie in terms of her likelihood of injury?"

Jett shrugged. "There's no guarantee about sporting injuries. Experienced athletes injure themselves every day. But I can assure you that as Sadie and I compete together, a high priority of mine will be keeping her safe. I definitely don't want both of us injured."

Sadie stepped closer to her dad and placed her hand on his cheek. "Daddy, I'll be fine. I have my class schedule all worked out. I'll do assignments on the trip up and back. I'll be on schedule to take my exam when I return. And I will be careful. You know me."

Shaw blinked and finally nodded his assent. "I know you. Determined daredevil, thrill-seeker." He glanced over at Jett. "My questions were only for my own comfort-level, not because I thought I could talk her out of it."

Jett chuckled. "I understand."

"Time to go," said Sadie. She bent and swiped a duffel bag from the floor, hoisting it over her shoulder. "Let's go do this thing."

Her dad gave her a hug. "Have fun. Be safe. Stay in touch."

She did a playful salute. "Got it."

In the truck, Jett reached behind to the back seat and pulled out a grocery bag full of snacks. "In case we get the munchies."

Sadie glanced in the bag. "Oh my gosh." She pulled out Oreos, Doritos and a plastic bottle of Pepsi. "I see you believe in health food and nutrients."

Jett laughed. "We'll need our energy on this trip."

They took off heading north for the fourteen-hour trip to Newport, Rhode Island. It would be a long day of driving, but tomorrow they'd rest and prepare the yacht for the race that started the following day. Sadie made herself comfortable in the passenger seat, then looked at him. "So, where's the boat?"

Jett chuckled. "Oh yeah, I forgot. We'll need the boat on this trip, won't we?"

She nudged his arm. "Seriously."

"I hire a yacht transport company when I have distant races. I worked with them yesterday afternoon to prep The Majestic, make sure she doesn't get banged up during the trip. Then we used the travel lift at the marina to haul her out and attach her to the trailer."

Sadie stared, her mouth open. "That sounds complicated. You somehow dragged that huge boat out of the water and onto a trailer to be driven eight hundred miles over land?"

"That's about the gist of it. Yep."

Sadie shook her head. "Amazing."

They drove mostly in silence, occasionally chatting, and then Sadie settled into her homework.

~ * ~

After a long drive and an exhausted sleep in a hotel room in Newport, Sadie awoke to a warm, bright June morning. She took ten minutes to perform stretches in her hotel room, then jumped in the shower. She and Jett had planned last night to meet for breakfast and then figure out where the boat was in transit.

Right on time, she entered the hotel lobby and saw Jett standing in the corner, tapping into his cell phone. "Hi."

He looked up. "Hey." He gestured with his phone. "The driver said they're about a hundred miles away. They should be here in a couple of hours."

"Great. No problems, I assume?"

"Nope. She's a good traveler." He grinned at her. "Hungry?"

They drove to a pancake house and Jett ordered the works: pancakes, eggs, sausage and fruit. Sadie chose a smaller but still filling meal of a vegetable omelet and yogurt. As they ate, they discussed the registration. It opened at nine this morning, so they'd head over there right after breakfast.

When the plates had been cleared and they were enjoying a second cup of coffee, Sadie said, "I don't know how you feel about this, but I'm thinking a prayer is in order." She lifted her head to study his face for his reaction.

"A prayer for what?" Jett asked.

She shrugged. "For a healthy, successful finish, and to achieve your goal of getting your contract."

Jett's face scrunched into an expression of doubt.

"Do you believe in the power of prayer?"

"Yeah, sure I do. But I don't know. Praying for no injuries is one thing. Praying for a safe sail. But praying for me to win the race to earn a big contract? That doesn't seem right. I mean, what if every sailor in there prayed for God to help him win the race? Only one prayer will be answered, right?"

Sadie quieted and thought for a moment. "Prayer is a two-way street. Praying for something is one side – the human asking for what he or she wants. Prayer is not complete until it's received by God. And God is only going to respond with His plan."

Jett nodded somberly. "So, you're saying we can ask, but we may not receive because it may not be God's plan."

"Exactly."

"So, why ask at all? I mean, God most likely has a plan for everyone. Whether or not we ask won't change what He planned to do all along, right?"

Sadie smiled and puffed out a breath. "Wow, this is getting deep fast. Not sure I was planning on theological discussions over breakfast."

Jett chuckled. "Never mind."

"No, actually I want to try to answer. At least, according to my views. That doesn't mean that it's right." Sadie thought for a moment. "There's a popular Bible verse in the Gospels, in Matthew, I think, that says, 'Ask and it will be given to you. Seek and you will find. Knock and the door will be opened to you.'"

Jett nodded. "I've heard of it. But that sort of contradicts your belief that you can ask, and you may not receive."

"I honestly don't think so. God wants us to ask him for our heart's desire. He invites us to include him in our daily lives, our decisions, the big ones and the small ones. But he knows better than we do. He sees the big picture, while we don't. By asking, we are including him into our lives. We may not get exactly what we asked for. But we are opening ourselves up to receiving his will." She ran a hand over her ponytail. "Does that make any sense at all?"

"Yeah."

Sadie examined his face to determine his comfort level with this discussion. "Do you pray?"

He paused. "Not like that, not like what you're talking about. I do pray for people who are sick or when they've lost someone dear to them. Mostly I pray when I'm scared or in trouble. When I know I can't fix it by myself." He looked thoughtful.

"Would you consider praying with me about our race?"

He shrugged. "Here?"

She looked around. "We can pray in your truck if you're more comfortable."

Nodding, he said, "Yeah, I don't really want to be on display."

They paid their bills and left. Settled in the truck, Sadie said, "I want you to know that I pray to God before every marathon I do. I pray for me to make good decisions, to stay healthy and avoid injury. I don't pray for a win because I know I have to put in more effort and training before I deserve to win. But I like knowing he's with me every step of the way."

Jett sat quietly. She hoped he was gaining comfort in the prayer concept. "Ready?" she asked. She closed her eyes and bowed her head. "Dear God, please be with Jett and me in the sailing race. Keep us safe, watch over us. Watch over all our competitors as well. Help us be successful in the race and earn Jett the Sailtone contract that he so richly deserves. We appreciate your love and support. Amen."

She sat in the silence of the truck and then opened her eyes. She looked over at Jett. He still had his head bowed, but he came out of the quiet and looked at her.

"Okay. We're all set."

She could tell from his tone that he was a little uncomfortable, but she sent a second, silent prayer to heaven that God would use her as a role model in Jett's spiritual life, a living example so he could examine his own relationship with God and reach for improvements.

On impulse, she reached out and placed her hands over his, squeezing them. "Every little bit helps, right?"

Chapter Nine

Shaw glanced at the clock in the kitchen, then headed out the back door. It was only ten minutes before Nora was due over for dinner. He trotted down the cement steps to the stone patio and gripped the cloth bag by the drawstring, then dragged it close to the water spicket. When he twisted the bag upside down, a peck of raw oysters cascaded out.

Turning on the water, he gave the oysters a hearty bath, removing the remnant mud. After all, these creatures had been living in the mud off the shore of Charleston just hours ago. The need to wash them was proof of their freshness.

Finishing the shower, he gathered the oysters and dropped them in a big tin basin. Placing it close to the grill, he grabbed two big sheets of burlap and soaked them too.

All ready for an Oyster Roast for Two. Nora was bringing side dishes and a peck of oysters would provide enough meat to feed them both.

On his way back up the steps to the house, the door opened, and out walked Nora carrying two glasses of sweet tea. With a big smile, he pulled her into an embrace while they both tottered on different level steps. She laughed, and they broke apart. He took a glass from her and took a big sip. "Hope you're hungry," he said.

"Oysters, huh?" she said dubiously, looking at what he'd set up. "You shouldn't have." She chuckled.

"I wasn't sure if you liked them, but I figured your Low Country experience wouldn't be complete until you savored an authentic oyster roast."

"So, you took it upon yourself to educate me. You couldn't just do a simple hamburger?"

He chuckled. "If you don't like oysters, I'll grill you a hamburger. But I'm guessing that you'll like these."

She shrugged. "My mom always said you have to at least try one bite, then decide. As long as I don't starve, I'm game."

"I'm honored to present you with your first oyster roast."

They walked over to the grill. Shaw picked up the basin of oysters and dumped them on the grill, taking care to distribute them evenly. He laid the first burlap over the big shells, then a second one, tucking it in around the sides. "The burlap helps them to steam inside there. The combination of grilling and steaming makes the most tender oysters."

"How long do you cook them?"

"Just a few minutes. Would you care to eat outside?" He gestured to the picnic table where he'd set plates and silverware.

"Sure. I'll get the sides and bring them out." She disappeared into the house and returned carrying a small platter containing four ears of corn, and a ceramic pot of baked beans. She removed the lid and the aroma of the beans drifted to his nose, making his stomach growl.

"This is a dinner fit for a king and queen," he said with a smile. "In fact, I believe the oysters should be ready. Have a seat and I'll bring them over."

He removed the burlap sheets, folded them roughly and placed them aside. With big oven gloves covering his hands, his lifted the grill from the fire and angled it so the oysters could slide into the tin basin. Carrying it over, he dumped about half the oysters onto the picnic table.

Nora laughed. "Oh, you spoil me. So fancy."

They sat, and Shaw demonstrated how to open the delicacy with an oyster knife. He'd cooked them long enough that many of them had popped open. Nora took her first bite and closed her eyes, savoring the unusual taste. Then she sighed with a "Mmmmmmm."

"Good?" he asked, amused at how much he wanted her to like it.

"Yes. It tastes like I would imagine the salt marsh to taste. Salty, fishy, gooey. But good."

He laughed. "I'll take it."

They dug into their meal, loading their plates up with corn and beans, and picking through the stack of oysters, digging the meat out, eating it, and tossing the empty shells into the basin. The township encouraged recycling of the empty oyster shells and provided spots to do so. He'd make sure to take them over later.

"Have you heard from Sadie?" Nora asked as they ate.

"I got a text. They arrived last night."

"Race is tomorrow?"

"Yeah."

"I'm so impressed with that young lady. Helping a friend achieve his own dreams, while attempting something she's never even done before."

Shaw nodded. "She's determined, that one."

"And generous. With her time and her skills."

"I agree with all that. She's helping this Jett fellow out, and that's kind of her. But she's also getting something she loves, which is a new adventure. She's a thrill seeker, and this is a thrill she's never experienced before. Racing a big sailing yacht in the ocean for eight hundred miles? Yes. Sadie would jump all over that."

When they'd put a huge dent in the oysters, they slowed down. It had been a delicious meal. They cleaned up and put the leftovers in the refrigerator. Shaw looked forward to a duplicate meal in a day or two.

He made decaf coffee and they sat together on the couch in the living room. Nora laid her head on his shoulder. "This is nice."

Shaw nodded. "It sure is."

"This is what our lives will be like as old married folks, huh?" She turned and gave him a contented smile.

"I suppose it is." Hard work that filled their souls with satisfaction during the day, delicious meals and relaxation in the evening. He looked forward to it.

"Maybe we should talk about our plans." She played with the ring on her finger and held it out to study. "I assume you'll move into my place after we marry?"

"Yeah, that makes the most sense. You've put so much work into renovating it. Your Dress for Success business is there, and Thunder lives in the barn. I'll probably hand this place over to Sadie to live in. If she ever wants to move, I'll put it up for sale."

Nora nodded slowly. "And when will that be?"

"When will I move in? After we get married."

Nora chuckled. "And when will *that* be?"

"Oh." Shaw smiled. "Tonight?"

She rose, turned and looked at him. "I know you're kidding, but ..."

"I'm only half kidding, Nora. I'm ready to marry you anytime. Start our new lives together. Be with you as man and wife. You tell me when and I'll be there."

She sat quietly. "Do you have any preferences about the wedding?"

"No."

"No long-held dreams about what you want for your wedding day?"

He pulled her close to rest against his chest. "Sure, I had a dream. I wanted to find a woman who made me happy, who made my heart race at the mere sight of her. I wanted a woman with goals and morals consistent with mine, someone who loved God, respected herself and wanted to spend her life with me. That was my dream. It came true the minute you said you'd marry me." She turned and looked into his eyes. "You are my dream, Nora. The rest? It's just gravy."

She leaned closer. Their kiss turned long and deep and passionate. She eventually pulled away. "I love you," she said breathlessly.

"I love you, too." The beating of her heart pounded against his as he held her tight. "How about you? Do you have any dreams about your wedding day?"

She paused. "Honestly, long ago I gave up the hope of finding the man of my dreams and marrying him. I figured I could either have a successful career or a successful marriage. But it didn't look like I was going to have both. Until I met you. Now it looks like I'm going to marry the love of my life, live in a place that makes my spirit sing, and perform important work that helps other people. The trifecta. I don't want a big, fancy wedding, because it'll just delay me getting to it."

"We could do something quick and simple."

"Yes. And tasteful. Memorable, but nothing fancy." She looked at him and laughed. "Sort of like us."

He pulled her back for another kiss, but he could tell her mind was working out the details. She ended the kiss and said, "How would you feel about an outdoor wedding in the pasture? I'll rent a wooden gazebo to stand under. We'll ask Pastor Ralph from the church to do the ceremony. And cake and punch in the house. We'll invite just a few close friends. Family. Sadie, my sister Patty. Maybe a dozen people. How does that sound to you?"

"It sounds perfect."

She stood, went to the kitchen and got a pad of paper out of a drawer. She came back, making notes. He'd lost her. She was absorbed in planning the wedding now. That was okay.

"It's going to be soon," she said, her pen to her mouth. "Why wait?"

"Exactly."

She went back to work and he suppressed a grin.

~ * ~

By mid-morning, The Majestic arrived in Newport and Jett worked with the transporter to unload her successfully from the trailer, dip her into her slip at the race marina, remove all her transport materials and assemble the tall masts in place. She looked good. Perfect, in fact. She'd survived the transport with all pieces intact. She was ready to sail tomorrow.

Sadie held a palm up to him and he slapped it, then gripped it before she could remove hers. "Sorry I wasn't more help with the unload," she said.

"No problem at all. Tomorrow is when I need you, and you'll be there for that."

She nodded. "I've sort of got the nervous stomach," she confessed.

Chuckling, he released her hand. "Good. I get one before every race. Means you know how important it is, and you're putting pressure on yourself to do well."

He knew she understood the concept. All competitive athletes recognized the balance between the pressure they put on themselves and the need to perform unencumbered. A tricky balance, but a necessary one.

They approached the line of tables set up on the dock within the marina. The hustle bustle was palpable. Hundreds of sailors milled around, most of them accompanied by their team members, wearing their signature colors emblazoned with the name of their vessel. Snatches of nervous laughter and excited conversation caught Jett's ear as they made their way to the registration table designated for the double-handed racers. Beautiful, graceful racing ships dotted the water behind them, each racer's investment carefully placed down in the water and babied with love.

Sailing competitors worked their entire lives to be here. Lifetimes of practice and knowledge of the sailing sport culminated in showings like this one. Jett felt honored to be here, and competitiveness soared within him. He deserved to be here. So much was riding on his appearance, and it wasn't limited to the Sailtone contract. Sure, he had agreed that he wouldn't get the lucrative sponsorship contract from the sailing product giant unless he placed in the top three. But there was more.

Respect from those who knew what it took to compete at this level. Admiration for his skills and dedication. Name recognition and a synonym for quality in the sailing world. From his fellow competitors, sure. But more importantly, from one man in particular he had sought approval from, his entire life. A strict disciplinarian and a hard sell.

His father.

Why did sons always strive to seek approval from the one man who had been with them from the very beginning? Who had seen them in their best moments and their worst? Did sons think they weren't truly successful unless their fathers gave them their stamp of approval?

What about when that father was the most highly-respected, highly-achieving man the son knew? How could a son possibly earn that father's respect?

"Hey, what's up with you?" Sadie's voice interrupted his thoughts, and he shook his head to wipe out the subject that dominated them.

A nudge from his partner brought a gentle smile to his face. No need for her to worry that he was spacing out. "Yeah, sorry." She gave him a quizzical gaze. "I'm fine," he assured her.

"You were literally a stone wall while I was talking to you. Did you hear a word I said?"

He held his mouth shut while studying her face, then decided honesty was the best way to go. "No, I didn't. Sorry. I was lost in my thoughts."

Her frown displayed her worry over his answer. He reached for her hand. "Won't happen again. I promise." And he would make sure it wouldn't happen again over the duration of the race. Dwelling on his father's disapproval of him was a topic that never served him well. It wasn't healthy, it wasn't productive. No matter what he did, his father would never approve of him. He imagined that even if he won this race, and the Sailtone contract, and made a million dollars with his own invention, there would still be plenty his father could pick at to communicate his disapproval of his only son.

"Done. Now, would you mind repeating what you said when I was ignoring you?" He flashed her his trademark carefree smile.

"I was just wondering about this registration process."

Jett shook his head. "Just a formality. We've been pre-registered for months online. Although I originally registered for the single-handed race, I called a race official when you joined me and got us switched to the double-handed division. This is just to pick up our tags and identification."

Their turn at the registration table finally arrived. "The Majestic for the double-handed race. Jett Martin, Skipper."

A young man with tanned skin and highlighted hair used his fingers to maneuver through the big manila envelopes in the box on the table in front of him, finally pulling one out. He flashed a smile, marked something on the master list in front of him and handed the packet to Jett. "There you are. Be here at eight tomorrow morning, ready to sail."

Jett took the envelope and glanced at it. "No, you gave me the wrong one. This one is for Cameron Martin. I'm Jett."

The young man apologized and dug back into the box.

"Common name, Martin," said Sadie.

Jett thought for a moment, then decided to come clean with her. "That's actually my father. Cameron Martin."

"You're kidding! Your father is competing here too?"

If she knew the level of contention between the two of them, she wouldn't be asking with that happy expression. "Yeah. When I moved from the single-handed to the double-handed event, it made us competitors."

Something in the tone of his voice must've alerted Sadie to the fact that this was not a happy coincidence. "Oh, Jett, I ...," she started, but a booming voice came from behind them, "There he is. The gym rat who thinks he can compete with the big boys in the sailing world."

Jett closed his eyes in frustration. Of course, he knew he'd have to face his father today or tomorrow. He was just hoping it would be later rather than sooner. He turned. "Hey, Dad."

His father reached out and tugged on Jett's long hair. "You look like a hippie, son. Can I give you a few bills for a haircut?"

Jett clamped his lips shut and let his eyes swing over his father's clean-shaven face and his crewcut hair. "Nope. Don't need your money, as you well know." The minute the words slipped out of his mouth, he regretted them. He didn't need to include Sadie in the ongoing feud between the two of them, especially when she had a normal father, one who loved and supported her.

"This is my sailing partner, Sadie Flynn." He stepped back after the introduction, allowing Sadie to shake his father's hand.

His father's gaze darted between Sadie and Jett. His impeccable manners to anyone outside the family won the moment, and he looked at Sadie, bowed slightly and shook her hand, saying, "So nice to meet you, young lady." Then he frowned at Jett. "Sailing partner? You told me you'd enrolled in the single-handed race. No partners allowed, son. Didn't they tell you that?"

Jett clenched his teeth. Spend much more time in his father's presence and he'd need dental work. Relaxing his jaw, he responded, "I've had a change of plans, Dad. Sadie and I are competing in the double-handed division."

His dad's mouth dropped open, and at least Jett could have the momentary satisfaction of causing his father to go speechless. Then he recovered with a cautious question in a menacing tone, "You're competing against me?"

"Looks like it," Jett responded casually, injecting his carefree smile to irritate his father further.

"Okay," said the young man at the registration table, holding out two identical envelopes. "I've got this worked out. Jett Martin, Captain of The Majestic, here's your registration packet. And Cameron Martin, Captain of The Wolverine, here's your registration packet. Sorry for the mix-up."

Jett and his dad took their packets and stepped away from the table. A few steps away from the crowd, Cameron got in one last typical dig, "I know you've never raced double-handed before, son. Instead of humiliating yourself and the Martin name, I hope you'll seek out some advice and guidance from your dear old dad."

Jett scratched his neck. "No need, Dad. Sadie and I will be fine. Good luck." He turned and strode away before he could get pulled in to his father's old tricks that he'd endured his whole life. He only hoped that Sadie had followed him and not stayed for further conversation. Turning his head, he was relieved to see she was right behind him. They walked to a bench and he sat, gesturing an invitation for her to join him.

They sat in silence. He fingered the corner of the envelope while his pulse slowed to a normal pace.

"That was your dad?" Sadie asked in a quiet voice. "I mean, obviously he is, but ... wow." Her concerned eyes sought out his face.

"Yeah, sorry about that. I knew he would be here, but I didn't know exactly how to prepare you. He's one of a kind."

Sadie's eyes went wide. "Uh, that's one way of saying it. What's his problem?"

Jett let out a laugh. "He can't stand me."

Sadie started to argue, then stopped. She put a comforting hand on his arm. "But why?"

"My dad is a high-ranking officer in the Air Force. He spent most of his time flying airplanes. He's an expert pilot."

Sadie looked down. "Pilot for his day job, sailor for his hobby. That's about as alpha male as you can get."

"Yeah. And I am his only son. His only child. To say that he had high expectations for me, would be an understatement."

Sadie reached for his hand and squeezed it. "And he thinks you didn't live up to them?" Her question caused his heart toward warm for her.

"Exactly."

"But you're an awesome son. I mean, obviously the two of you don't get along, but you've made a success of your life. What is his problem with you?"

He turned on the bench, so he was facing her. "He wanted me to do exactly what he did. Play team sports, go to college, become a military officer. Ever wonder why my name is Jett?"

She blinked. "No, not really. I figured it was a nickname."

"He wanted me to be a fighter pilot. He'd made that decision in utero."

She gave him a grim grin. "Wow."

"I bucked him at every turn. We established a relationship early on that if he wanted me to do something, I strove to do the exact opposite. We're both stubborn, just in different ways. I didn't do any of that stuff he wanted me to do, so he thinks my whole life is a failure."

Protective anger flared in her eyes. "Doesn't he know what a great athletic trainer you are? How strong you are? Hard-working? Great with people? What about your invention? Isn't he proud of that?"

Jett shook his head. "He doesn't know about any of that. I don't share the details of my life with him. I stay as far as I can away from him."

They sat quietly, then Sadie stood in front of him and placed her hands on his shoulders. "Well, may the best man win."

Jett chuckled. Could he even dream of beating his father in this race? No, he decided. That didn't matter. His goal was to place in the top three for the sake of the contract, not some revenge match to pummel his father. He needed to push that out of his mind right now.

He rose. Sadie said, "Do you need me for anything right now? I've got a couple free hours to do homework if not."

He waved his hand. "Go."

"I'll be in my room. Come get me if you need me." She gave him a wave and turned in the direction of the hotel.

He watched her walk away, then headed for the boat. He'd checked it twice already, but no harm in checking again. Besides, on deck was where he felt most happy and confident. His daddy-driven insecurities never hit him there. Good thing too, since he didn't need his dad in his brain while he was competing. Just his instincts.

As he strode toward the boat, he remembered the prayer Sadie had led him in at the diner this morning. God wanted to hear from him. In his time of need, in his time of celebration, at all times. It was a new concept to him, but in light of tomorrow's challenges, it certainly couldn't hurt to call on the Almighty.

"Dear Lord," he murmured to himself, "please be with us tomorrow. Keep us safe and help us to work together as a team. Watch over Sadie as she helps me with this race. Watch over me too. Amen."

Chapter Ten

The next morning presented them with a magnificent sunny New England day, custom-made for virtually any outdoor activity, but especially sailing. Sailors checked the weather incessantly, and Jett had been checking the forecast for a week straight now, but the reality of this day was better than his fondest fantasy.

He tapped on Sadie's hotel room door at seven o'clock, his excitement displayed in the speed of his heart rate. This was the day. It was finally here.

Sadie opened the door and the first thing he saw was a beaming smile. She surprised him by pulling him into a hug. He closed his eyes and breathed in the scent of her hair. Lemon, if he wasn't mistaken. His new favorite aroma.

"Couldn't have ordered a better day for sailing, I assume," she said, pulling back and smiling up at him, a picture of cheerfulness and beauty.

"You're right about that. Great day for a launch."

She pulled her duffel bag over her right shoulder and stepped out, closing the door behind her. "I'm ready."

They rode the elevator down and took a moment to check out of the hotel. They drove to the marina. While he was concentrating on finding a parking spot, Sadie let out an appreciative whistle.

"Wow, look at this place. Unbelievable."

He tried to see it through her eyes, a first-timer to the world of competitive yacht sailing. It certainly was impressive. People milling around the pier, some dressed in matching uniforms for the multi-crewed teams. The blue of the water contrasting with the blue of the sky, dotted with puffy white clouds. And the yachts. The magical, majestic yachts with the tall sails. A sport for kings, a luxurious sport, but requiring energy and expertise.

He smiled over at her. "Yep. Welcome to your first yacht sailing race."

After parking, Sadie grabbed his hand as they walked to the slip. They had a couple hours to go before the official start of the race, but they had a few tasks to complete: pack away the food they'd need for the race, double and triple check the equipment, and download the race's software to the ship's computer equipment to ensure they were on track with the route.

At ten o'clock, they had maneuvered The Majestic out of the slip and had joined their competitors at their designated spot facing the "starting line," which for a yacht race, was a virtual line in the water, between a buoy on one side, and a motorboat holding the race committee, responsible for shooting off the starting gun. Jett's first job as skipper of this race was determining his starting mark strategy. His goal was to make a clean start in a competitive position without breaking any of the right-of-way rules. With all the boats competing for a front-row start, he had to assess the favored position, whether that be a front-row start in the middle of the pack or at the favored end of the line.

"Racers," boomed a magnified voice that all the sailors could hear, "twenty seconds till start, double-handed division."

"Time to go," Jett called to Sadie. She nodded and positioned herself in the center of the deck, ready to quickly reposition based on his order. All her sheets were clean, no tangles, all looped in neat circles and out of the way for a clear work space. Their gazes connected, her excited smile assuring him that she was ready.

Assessing the approach to the starting line, he determined the favored end of the line was the starboard side. Based on the direction the wind was blowing, his first order would be to position the sails into the wind and tack to the port.

"Ready to tack," he called to Sadie.

"Ready," Sadie said, understanding the order, but waiting for his next command that would tell her to do it.

The Majestic sailed over the imaginary starting line in great position and Jett let out a whoop. "Tacking!" he yelled.

Sadie jumped into action. While he watched, she released the starboard jib sheet to tack to starboard. Then she took in the port sheet to complete the tack. "Done."

"Great job," he praised her and held up a thumb. Her face flushed at his compliment.

"Now what?" she asked.

"I'll watch our course and our progress, and I'll let you know when we need to adjust direction."

Sadie stood in the center of the boat and tilted her head back, looking up the mast. "The wind's strong. The sails are really pulling."

"Enjoy it while it lasts. If the winds decrease, our speed slows down too."

The first hour of the race cleared out the pack. Captains of each yacht had charted a course, and although they were all heading for the same destination, there were optimal choices in how to get there. While all twenty-some competitors in their division had started together, by the second hour, there were fewer yachts within sight. By the third hour, they were virtually alone in the sea.

"Ready for lunch?" he called to Sadie.

She pulled her attention away from the sea. "Okay."

He went below deck and made two sandwiches, grabbed a bag of chips and returned to the deck. They sat and ate, surrounded by the sweep of the wind, the sun's strong rays and the infinite splash of the ocean's waves.

"It's gorgeous out here," said Sadie.

"My thoughts exactly. People talk about their happy place, the place where they are most truly happy and content. This is it for me. Out here."

She glanced over at him. "Some people strive their entire lives to find what makes them happy. You're lucky to have discovered it."

As he gazed at her, his thoughts revisited old ground: what a perfect match she was for him. They were alike in so many ways. Different, as well. Sadie was a high achieving student. She would be a success at whatever she put her mind to. He didn't have her drive for schooling and career, but in athletics, they were the same.

He set his empty plate aside and reclined on the bench, then grimaced at the stab of pain in his rib. Instead he sat up straight.

"Let me know if you need me to do anything," said Sadie.

Jett stood. "Come on below deck and I'll show you the electronics."

They climbed down the narrow staircase to the cabin. It was small but capable of seating a half dozen people. It featured a couple of bunks, a restroom and a tiny shower, as well as a small kitchen. Every inch of space was designed for maximum usefulness.

Jett led her to the computer and the radio. "I want you to know how to call for help, just in case you need to know."

Her eyes widened, and he knew she understood his meaning. "If for some reason I can't call for help, you'll know how."

She nodded gravely. He went through the steps to use the radio.

"But, I want you to know, Sadie, if we have to call for help, we're disqualified from the race. A call for help means we can't compete anymore."

Sadie studied his face in silence.

"Now, this is the navigation system. I charted a course, and I'll check it periodically to make sure we're staying on track as planned. If we go off course, we'll be able to more easily get back on track using this software." He showed her the basics of the system.

"Take your pick of bunks," he said, gesturing with an arm. "During the night we'll each take three-hour shifts to sleep."

That news surprised her. "What? I'll be out there all by myself with the yacht in the middle of the night?"

His grin formed slowly on his face. "Well, yeah. You didn't think I'd be able to stay awake twenty-four seven for four days, did you?"

She grimaced. "I didn't really think about it, but yeah, I guess not." "You'll be fine."

They returned to the deck and Jett made some adjustments to the sails. Then they rested. Long-term sailing races required a lot of judgment and spurts of activity, cushioned with long periods of inactivity. The difference with this race was, he had a partner. Sadie would help him pass the long hours.

~ * ~

The day had passed relatively peacefully for Sadie. After the thrill of the start, they had been sailing solidly all day. Every once in a while, Captain Jett would order an adjustment in direction, moving the sails here or there, correcting course. Sometimes he'd climb partway up the mast to look farther out on the horizon, or he'd go below-deck to study his navigation software. Sadie had all the faith in him in the world.

They watched the sun set. Sadie snapped a shot with her cell phone. The colors were gorgeous, and the uninterrupted vista provided a phenomenal view. This was how God intended sunsets to look, before humans started building encroachments on the horizon.

"Did you ever think about how many sailors across the expanse of history have looked at this same exact view?" She glanced at Jett. "Christopher Columbus may have traveled this same bit of ocean and seen this same exact sunset, almost six hundred years ago."

Jett smiled. "I've never really thought of it like that. But yeah, that's true. Very few parts of the world look exactly the same over six hundred years."

Around nine o'clock, Jett said, "Why don't you go catch a nap in your bunk now? Try to sleep and I'll come get you at midnight."

Although she couldn't remember the last time she'd gone to bed this early, Sadie didn't argue. "Aye aye, Captain," she said, and climbed below deck.

Settling into her bunk, she tried to clear her mind. She was with Jett, just the two of them in the middle of nowhere. Despite her determination to keep it platonic between the two of them, she kept noticing traces of physical attraction to him. He was extremely good-looking; she'd always known that. It was evident to anyone looking at him. Fit, strong, happy, carefree smile, hair that made her want to run her hands through it, eyes that crinkled when he laughed.

But it wasn't just physical. She admired him. His knowledge, his abilities, his solid decision-making during the course of this race. She was in good hands under his tutelage. He was performing at the top of his game. Doing the thing he did best ... sailing ... and that was very attractive.

She turned over onto her side and closed her eyes, but her thoughts weren't finished yet.

Was this how her mother had felt about her dad when they'd first met? Did she sneak glances at him working, and feel a flush of attraction flood through her body? She must've thought her dad was the one true love for her, or she wouldn't have married him, right?

Or, had her mother fallen in love with the idea of being in love, and hadn't been diligent about finding the exact right person to match her goals and dreams. Her father was a superb human being, but he was not a good fit for the woman he married. Their mismatch was evidently obvious right away. It was no secret to anyone that they'd rushed into marriage, and the result was disastrous, every single day of their entire lives.

They wanted different things, and they both pursued what they wanted, despite the other not being on board.

The marriage was over long before it ended. And if there was one thing Sadie learned from growing up in the midst of it, she would never, ever make the same mistake her parents did. She would never allow herself to fall in love with the wrong person. She would much rather not have love at all, than settle for the wrong love. Making a mistake of that magnitude would ruin everything she'd built in her life.

So where did that leave her and her growing feelings for Jett? Should she shut them down now, slam the fortress door shut to her heart?

Or, should she explore where her feelings took her? Should she depart from her normal path and consider a relationship with this man? Open herself up to a potential misstep, but meanwhile enjoy the fun and companionship that she'd always deprived herself of that a relationship might provide?

The possibility made her body respond in a variety of ways. Fear of the unknown, opening herself to a new path she'd always forbidden before. And curiosity, the excitement of plunging into unknown territory. Maybe she was ready, even though she had no idea how to start.

Reaching an impasse with her thoughts, she took control and shut them down, closed her eyes and concentrated on sleep.

Chapter Eleven

The second day of sailing went smoothly. Jett was fully in captain mode, watching the boat's progress across the sea, making judgment calls about the positioning of the sails to maximize wind power and speed, studying the course software to determine if an optimization was possible to cut off time.

"Jett! Look!" Sadie's excited voice came to him on the wind and he turned to find her. She stood on the starboard side, pointing into the water. He looked and saw four or five dolphins swimming alongside them, jumping playfully over the waves generated by his yacht.

"Yeah!" he laughed. "Dolphins are great companions. Just so we don't run into any sharks."

"Don't jinx us!" yelled Sadie.

Later in the day, they sat on the benches rimming the interior of the boat, facing each other. Sadie had brought out her schoolwork, and was reading a big textbook. She set it aside, looked at him, and said, "I was thinking about your dad."

He coughed. "What? Why?"

She shrugged and brought her feet up on the bench beside her. "What makes him tick? Most fathers are supportive of their children. Encourage them to succeed. What went wrong with your dad?" Her eyes went wide as she glanced his way. "I'm sorry. Does this topic hurt your feelings?"

He lifted one shoulder and let it drop. "No. I've long ago given up on the idea of my father and I having a healthy father/son relationship."

"That's sad," she said. "Don't give up on him."

Jett let his gaze rest on her face. Give up on his dad? That was a new way of looking at it. He'd always figured his dad had given up on him, and never thought of it the other way around. "I imagine your own dad is loving and supportive and encouraging. That's your life experience. But don't fool yourself into thinking that's how all fathers are."

She frowned. "Maybe you're right. I'm extremely sheltered because my own dad is so great. But I had a mother who couldn't care less about me, or him. She couldn't be bothered with mothering. My dad was really my mother and father. She wasn't abusive though. Just absent."

"My dad was absent a lot while I was growing up. He was deployed for months at a time. When he came back, he wanted to force me into a box, based on what he wanted my interests to be. But I wasn't about to let this stranger come and mess up the life I had at home. Try as he might, he couldn't bully me into being the kind of kid he had in mind."

"Well, that's good. Even he should be able to see the strength you showed in that decision. He should actually admire you for being true to yourself instead of caving to what he wanted."

Jett shook his head. "No, he never actually got there. He wasn't exactly self-aware." He shifted positions to avoid his rib becoming painful. "Things just got worse as I got older. I was more rebellious, he was more angry. Oil and water, the two of us. I couldn't wait to get out of high school and out of that house."

Sadie shook her head sadly. "So, he's let his anger turn him into a hateful person toward you. No empathy or well wishes on your accomplishments, because you ended up different than his plans for you."

"I guess. To be honest, I'd rather avoid him than try to figure him out. Or, God forbid, reform him."

"How's your mom?"

"She's good. Still married to him, so I don't see her much either. But we stay in touch. Phone calls, texts. I don't know how she's stayed with him all these years. But at least she loves me."

They sank into a comfortable silence and Jett realized he'd never spoken to a woman about his father before, never dug this deep into his thoughts and feelings about his father's treatment of him. There was something special about Sadie.

On the second night, he'd taken the nine to midnight shift while Sadie slept. Things were going smoothly, and he'd bathed the entire boat in light. They were in the middle of nowhere, no land visible in any direction, but thanks to the navigation software, he knew exactly where they were. It was a good time to hand the wheel over to Sadie and grab a couple hours' sleep.

He went below deck, and holding his hands in front of him, he made his way in the dark to Sadie's bunk. The lemon scent of her hair reached his nostrils and he paused to breathe it in. Her steady breathing made him regret the need to wake her out of a sound sleep. She'd been working hard as first mate, and he was pleased with her performance. She was a natural and he hoped she would continue sailing long after this race was over.

His thigh bumped into her bunk and he sat to avoid falling. Once there, he knew he should quickly stand so he wasn't invading her privacy. Joining her on her bunk struck him as inappropriately intimate.

And yet, he couldn't bring himself to leave. Instead, he leaned silently closer, enjoying the sight of her sleeping peacefully, his eyes adjusting to the dark. Her long brown hair covered the pillow in strands and she'd pulled the sheet up to her chin. She was a beautiful woman, kind and generous, and she'd rescued him from having to withdraw from this race and forfeit the Sailtone contract for good.

She was his savior. She'd said yes when all those better suited to help had said no. He owed her for this kindness. He just didn't know how to repay her.

She stirred, and he quickly came to his feet, not wanting her to find him sitting there. "Sadie?" he said quietly.

"Hmmmm," she murmured, turned her back to him and pulled the sheet up tighter.

He reached out cautiously and tapped her on the shoulder. She immediately sat straight up. "My turn?"

"Yeah. Sorry to wake you."

"No, it's my turn. Good." She flipped the sheet off her, and Jett saw that she'd slept in her swimsuit covered by shorts and t-shirt.

She glanced at him and he turned away, not wanting to intrude.

"How's it looking?"

"Good. Smooth sailing."

She rose out of bed, brushed her hair out of her face and went to the refrigerator. Extracting a bottle of water, she swallowed a swig and looked at him. "Ready."

He chuckled. "You get ready faster than any woman I've met in my life."

She shrugged. "Who am I going to see out here in the middle of nowhere?"

"Good point. Let me show you the map before you go up there." He pointed to their position on the screen and to where he hoped they'd reach by the end of her shift.

She nodded. "Anything tricky coming up?"

"Nope. Just say true. Keep her on course. Let me know if you have questions."

She climbed the stairs to the deck and he laid in his bunk. Last night, he'd stayed with her to get her settled during her shift, but she'd done well. Tonight, he didn't feel the need to accompany her. She'd do fine. He grabbed his phone, set the alarm for three o'clock, and worked on getting his mind settled for sleep.

A thudding sound was the first to wake him.

Then, a terrible scraping as the boat hull underneath him shuddered. He sat straight up in his dark bunk.

Then Sadie's scream, calling his name.

He rose and ran above deck, ignoring the jab of pain in his side. Sadie flew into his arms, sobbing. "Something happened! What happened?"

He flew into action, holding her firmly away by her shoulders. "We hit something. Let me check it out."

Grimacing at the pain searing through his ribs, he made his way up the mast, climbing step by step until he could look down at the black inky water. He flipped on a beam of light, moving it around, continuing to search. He half expected to see a partially submerged 55-gallon drum bobbing around in the ocean. They were often a concern in the open seas, did a bit of damage, but not enough to stop their progress in the race.

Unfortunately, it wasn't a bobbing drum he saw. The change in the water's color was enough to make his stomach clench with dread. That, and Sadie's shout: "Jett! Come down here!"

He made his way down the mast ladder and followed her voice below deck.

"I hear something I hadn't heard before," she said, faced him and pointed.

He slid to his knees and placed his ear along the wall of the cabin. A hissing of air, along with the sound of water dripping. His worst fears were confirmed.

"We've scraped against a coral reef. We've done some damage to the underbelly of the boat."

Sadie's eyes went wide, and she gasped. "What? We're going to sink?"

The last thing he needed was for his first mate to panic. He stood and grabbed her upper arms. "No, we're not going to sink. We're going to patch the hole and continue on."

She went silent and motionless. Then, with a tiny voice, "Does this happen often?"

He stared into her eyes. He wished he could lie to her, but he didn't have it in him. He had to be honest; they were a team. He'd tell the truth and then they'd work themselves through the consequences. Sailing wasn't always smooth; in fact, often it wasn't. This was a challenge they'd need to work through and move on. "No, this isn't common. But we can fix it."

"Jett," she said, her body shaking, "I'm so sorry. I did this. It was on my watch. I ran the boat over a coral reef. Now I've damaged your boat and ruined your chance of winning the race." Tears welled in her eyes.

He had to stop her crying. Not only did he need her help, but he couldn't bear to see her cry. "No, not at all. The coral reef was unexpected. Let's study the navigation system and we'll come up with a plan. But Sadie," he squeezed her arms and brought her close, "don't fall apart on me. I need you, understand?"

She gulped and nodded. She got it. She may not have been in this situation before, but he was positive she'd been in something similar. Losing control of her emotions would help no one.

They stepped over to the computer and he immediately saw the problem. "Okay, the wind blew us off course. We're east of where we want to be."

She sniffed. "I'm so sorry."

"No, it's okay. Remember? We're going to fix this. We'll be okay." Because they were closer to the shore than he'd set the course for, they had sailed over the top of a coral reef. He knew he had some patching to do on the underside of the hull. The question was, how big? Several times, he had patched a hole in the hull several inches long, and fortunately it was possible to apply the patch while still in the water. But he'd have to get underwater and put eyes on the hole before he could determine if they could finish the race. Time was of the essence. They had not a moment to waste.

He needed a plan, and he needed it fast.

~ * ~

Helplessness.

It was a feeling she'd never experienced before, and certainly not a feeling she liked. Sadie was always in charge of her life, of her schedule, of her goals. But riding a sinking boat in the middle of night, in the middle of the ocean with no land in sight, without the skills or knowledge to resolve it ... talk about being out of her comfort zone. *Way* out.

She watched Jett as he made his way around the cabin, opening cabinets and pulling out supplies. She suspected he was putting on an optimistic front for her sake, or did he truly feel this was a temporary setback and they'd be back on course soon? Were they both going to die out here in the dark ocean? Had she ruined this beloved yacht that had been in Jett's family forever?

She had no business being first mate in a race of this caliber. Jett may not have been able to compete without her, but he would at least still have an intact boat.

Jett approached her, hands full of supplies. "Here's the plan. I'll go underwater and locate the hole caused by the coral reef. Then I'll determine if I can patch it."

Sadie let out a troubled breath. "And what if we can't?"

His lips curled. "If I can patch it and keep the boat afloat we won't ever have to worry about Plan B. Let's go with this first, okay?"

She studied his face. "Why don't we use the radio to call for help, Jett? There's most likely a hole in the bottom of our boat. This seems like an insurmountable problem to handle without help."

"No!" He dumped the supplies on a countertop and grabbed her hands, shaking them urgently. "No, don't do that. The minute we call for help, we forfeit from the race."

Sadie raised her eyebrows at him. Forfeiting seemed the only logical course of action.

"Let's keep trying. Let's not give up, okay?"

"I'm so ....," she started but he stopped her.

"No. I shouldn't have given you that shift. I realize that now. Let's put that behind us and figure this out."

She cursed the tears that had appeared in her eyes. She wished she knew what she was doing. She wished she didn't have to rely on Jett to fix her mistake. But despite all her regrets, she wouldn't be a whimpering female whom he had to comfort. She refused to be that.

She pushed back her shoulders and lifted her chin. "Okay, tell me what you want me to do."

He gave her a grave nod and turned back to the supplies he'd placed on the counter. He lifted a small oxygen tank and a facemask.

"You have diving gear?" she asked, hope popping into her chest. She'd taken diving lessons. She'd completed a few training dives. She knew more what she was doing with scuba diving than sailing. She could help. "Do you have two masks and tanks?"

He shook his head. "I'll only need one," he replied, and with that, he swung the straps of the oxygen tank around his shoulders. And he shouted out with pain. She cringed at his outburst. "Dang it," he muttered.

"I'll do it," Sadie said decisively, and took the tank from him. It was heavy, but she'd carried one before on her back, and besides, when you were underwater, it didn't feel heavy at all. She got it strapped on tightly and held her hands out, demonstrating. "No problem. I've dove before. I can help."

Emotions flitted across his expression and she knew he struggled with putting her in danger, relying on her to do something he would normally do, admitting to his injury's restrictions on his body. He rubbed his broken rib gently and scowled. "I have a couple of diving masks, just the one tank. I'll come down with you and hold the beam, so you can see what you're doing. I'll have to hold my breath and surface to grab new air when I run out."

She nodded, a small smile on her face. Very little to smile about here, but at least she was helping to fix the problem she'd caused.

Jett held up a plastic tube, like a Jimmy Dean sausage roll. Opening it, he squeezed out a little fingerful of putty. "This stuff works miracles. It's water resistant, it's pliable and it stops the flooding." He extended his finger with the putty towards her. "Give it a try."

She took the putty and massaged it between her fingers. It was, just as Jett said, pliable and thick. It could be moved in any direction and formed into any shape.

"I've fixed many a hole in a hull with this stuff," said Jett.

"Strong enough to finish the race?" she asked, allowing herself an ounce of hopefulness.

"Quite possibly. It depends on what I see down there. Let me go down and examine the hole."

"I'm coming with you."

"Okay. First, we need to lower the sails, and anchor the boat. We definitely don't want to be doing this while we're moving."

She took the tank off, leaving it below deck, then up top, followed Jett's instructions to lower the sails. Jett took the helm. She looked at him curiously.

"There's some steps to follow to release the anchor. If you don't mind, I won't teach you right now. Time is of the essence and we need to secure the boat and start patching that hole."

"No problem." She agreed with him; she didn't need to know how to do it. The fact that he knew, and was physically able to accomplish the tasks required, was enough. Soon, Jett had the yacht anchored to his satisfaction and for the first time in two days, the boat was still. Jett made his way below deck and selected a diving mask that covered his eyes and nose. He also grabbed a high-beam flashlight. Coming above again, he lowered a ladder off the port side of the boat, so they could easily get in and out of the water.

Now, Sadie's turn at preparations. Jett assisted her with putting on the oxygen tank and her mask, and within minutes, she was set to begin using it underwater.

Last, Jett took a quick look below deck to see if the boat was taking on water. So far, so good. They still heard the sounds of water dripping and air fizzing in the interior, but the water was not making its way into the yacht yet.

They descended the ladder and as soon as they landed in the water, Sadie shivered. She had no idea what the water temperature was, but it was safe to say it was chilly. Jett flipped on his beam and the underside of the hull came into full view. Using his hands to guide him, Jett followed the surface of the hull, pointing the light, until he came to the damaged area. It was located on the bottom of the hull, so to patch it, Sadie would need to be directly beneath the boat. Jett held up a palm, like a stop sign, then surfaced before coming back. Sadie understood. *Stay here, while I get more air.*

On his return, Jett examined the damage. He pulled a cloth out of his pocket and wiped the surface clean, then kneaded the hole carefully with his fingers. Then he looked at Sadie and made an upwards gesture with his thumb before he ascended to the surface. She followed him. They met back at the ladder.

"Good news. It's not too bad. This putty should work, and I'm hopeful we'll be able to finish the race. Maybe every twelve hours or so I'll check it to see if it needs a touch up."

Sadie's heart jumped. "That's great, Jett!" Her conscience eased a tiny bit. Yes, she'd messed up. She'd caused them to go off course, adding time to their route, and worst of all, damaging his valuable boat.

But maybe? Maybe they were still in the game. She didn't even want to ask him. She'd just say a quick prayer and remain hopeful.

Jett pulled the tube of putty out of his pocket and handed it to her. "Here's where you come in. This could take five or six minutes, so you'll need to breathe with the tank. It's basically like Play-doh. Take a big blob of it, cover the hole, then spread it all around with your fingers. Up, down, to the right and the left. Don't worry about making it neat and pretty, just functional. Do whatever you can to fill the hole."

Sadie nodded. Seemed easy enough. She'd do her best.

"I'll come down and shine the beam, but when I go up for breaths you'll need to work in the dark for twenty seconds or so."

Sadie pushed that thought out of her mind ... positioned underneath a big yacht in the dark open seas ... no, she would not let fear take hold of her on that one. This was a new adventure. "Let's go."

They dove under the water, and Sadie positioned herself under the boat's hull, and with Jett's light illuminating the surface, she immediately went to work. She tugged a big piece of the putty out of the package and pushed it up against the hole. As Jett had instructed, she used her fingers to knead and push the goop into position. Taking a little more putty, she added it on top and stretched and kneaded. Suddenly she was in complete darkness. Jett must've gone up for air. She pushed words of comfort through her mind, *Lord, be with me in times of darkness, in times of uncertainty, in times of danger. Lead me safely to the light.*

As Jett had prepared her for, the light returned in less than half a minute. He was back with a new lungful of air. She continued to work the putty over the hole, stretching it over the damage. It appeared to be watertight but sitting still in the water was one thing. They needed it to be watertight while cutting at fast speeds through the ocean. She glanced down at the package in her hand and pulled a little more putty out so she could apply a second layer.

A powerful force thrusted into her from behind, and she lost her grip on the putty package. Gasping deeply in surprise, she moved her head just enough to catch a glimpse of the package disappearing into the sea below. A stab of disappointment rushed through her. What had happened? What had shoved her and made her drop the important stuff?

A faint alarm went off on her oxygen tank. Gasping like she had was not the proper way to breathe. Breathing underwater was all about regular, even breaths; even the most novice of divers knew that. The tank was reminding her to calm down and breathe regularly.

She forced her attention to her breathing, but it was quickly forgotten. Her next glimpse was of a shark, heading her way.

Chapter Twelve

Jett grabbed several deep breaths, held one, and lowered himself underwater. He pointed the beam of light onto the boat's hull where Sadie was working. Even several seconds of complete darkness could be frightening for someone not used to it, so he wanted to bathe her work area with light and remove any trace of nervousness, so she could finish the job.

What he didn't expect to see was an ocean predator making its way closer to her. He let out a yell, releasing the lion's share of air he'd just gathered into his lungs.

Flinging into action, he pushed off the boat's surface and propelled himself closer to Sadie. As he approached, the shark brushed against her, shoving her forward. He reached Sadie and grabbed her arm. Her head pitched in his direction and her eyes through the diving mask were terrified and wide.

He had to get her out of the water. He would fight the shark if he had to, and he'd learned some techniques for that, in his years of sailing, but removing Sadie from danger was his number one priority.

He pulled her toward him and wrapped his arm around her waist. She didn't fight him, in fact, she went soft like a rag doll. Maybe she'd passed out; he didn't know. As he squeezed her, a shot of pain from his ribs made him scream again out loud. His own pain didn't matter. Sadie was only here because he'd begged her to join him. A shark attack was not going to happen on his watch.

He turned toward the ladder, mere feet away, holding on to his first mate. He kicked his legs and swam with one arm. The shark approached menacingly close. He pointed the beam of light directly in the shark's eyes, giving him a few seconds of time as the shark pivoted and swam away. Jett reached the ladder and with all the strength he could muster, he pushed Sadie's body onto it.

He needed her to grip the handle and climb the ladder on her own. But she didn't.

He shook her and reached for her head, turning her neck so he could gaze into her face. Her eyes were closed.

"Sadie!" he yelled, but underwater, his voice barely made a sound. He shook her again, trying to awaken her back to consciousness.

The shark made its return trip. The beast propelled closer through the dark water. Positioning Sadie behind him on the ladder, he pushed his back up against her to protect her the best he could. Then, securing himself with his legs, he lifted the big flashlight with two hands above his head. Out of breath, an unconscious partner and a menacing shark patrolling, ready for the kill, he timed his attack. One, two, three. When the shark was within arm's reach, he lowered the flashlight on its head as hard as he could.

The flashlight fell out of his hands, losing the all-important light in the dark sea. The shark stilled. Jett used the last of his energy to throw Sadie over his shoulder and climb out of the sea.

He climbed the ladder, pain searing through his side, and lowered Sadie as gently as he could on the boat's deck. He grabbed air into his lungs. He hopped over the side and kneeled beside her, ripping off her face mask and tank so he could see her.

Her complexion was devoid of color, a ghostly white. He began massaging her cheeks and forehead with his fingers, moving to her neck and arms. All while words tripped off his tongue, "You're gonna be okay, Sadie, come on girl, I love you, I love you, Sadie." His brain wasn't engaged, he didn't even think about his words, he just let them come while he worked to revive this amazing young woman.

He checked her pulse and her heart beat. They were faint, but she was breathing. Hating to leave her, he bolted to his feet and ran below deck long enough to pull a blanket off his bunk. Returning, he draped it over her, tucking it in around her to provide instant warmth. "Sadie, come on now, come on back, you're okay."

A cough erupted from her, then her eyes opened, and she focused on him. The first word she said was, "Shark!"

He let out a hearty laugh, pure happiness and relief emerging from within him. She was okay. She was alive and fine. He wrapped his arms around her and pulled her, blanket and all, into an embrace. He buried his face in the curve of her neck and her hair covered his nose, breathing in that faint scent of lemon from her last shower. "You're okay," he muttered. "You're fine," probably as much to assure himself as her.

Eventually she pulled away. "What happened?" Her eyes sought his out, darting back and forth between the two of them. "I saw the shark and I don't remember anything else. Except, oh! I dropped the putty. The putty's gone, Jett. I'm sorry."

Unbidden laughter left his lips again. "Who cares about the putty? Don't worry about it."

She shook her head. "I got one layer on, but I was going to do another one when Jaws showed up. It won't hold. It won't be enough, Jett."

He lifted his hands and rested them gently on her face, covering her cheeks and jaws. "That doesn't matter. Nothing matters, Sadie, except that you're okay. That's an answer to my prayers. Thank you, God," he ended in a shout, his head back. "Thank you for saving Sadie!"

Sadie took a deep breath and let it out. "Tell me what happened."

He released her face and sought out her hands, taking them in his. "I went up for breath and came back down and saw the shark. Just then, he bumped you, so you saw him too. I grabbed you and got you to the ladder, but you must've fainted because you couldn't climb on your own."

"Oh my gosh, so how did you get me up the ladder?"

"I used my flashlight to hit ole Jaws in the face, then carried you up."

Her mouth dropped open. "You attacked a shark in open sea and carried me up a ladder with a broken rib?"

He stammered as her words sank in. When she put it like that, she made him sound like Superman. He'd just wanted to keep her safe. Maybe adrenaline had kicked in. It didn't matter. All that mattered at this moment was her. He brought a hand underneath her hair, cupped her jaw and placed his lips on hers. She shivered, and he used his free arm to pull her closer, to warm her, to give him a better angle for this essential kiss.

When she returned his passion, a stream of warmth flooded him, and he could only hope she felt it too. Their kissing magnified, under the stars, afloat on the vast ocean, the tall mast looking over them on deck of The Majestic while a shark circled around them.

He ended the kiss with a smile, leaning his mouth into her ear, and whispered, "I'd fight more than a shark and a broken rib to keep you safe."

She giggled, and he did too, and soon they separated, both lying back on the deck, laughing out loud. "So corny," she said between rips of laughter. They laughed till they could laugh no more, and laid on the deck, waiting for their breathing to get back to normal.

She sat. "Do you have more putty?"

He shrugged. "I can look. But I don't think so."

She wiped her cheek. "Will we have to withdraw?"

"No. Not unless we absolutely have to. This baby would have to be practically capsized before I admit defeat."

"Okay." Her voice was tiny. "What do we do now?"

"I think we could both use some rest. Why don't we keep her anchored and we both go to our bunks and get some sleep?"

"You're the captain."

They rose and descended the stairs, finding their bunks in the darkness. Jett settled into his and listened for the sounds of Sadie settling into hers. "Good night," he whispered.

"Night."

He listened to her breathing until he thought it had evened into slumber. Then he closed his eyes and allowed himself to drift off. But her voice came to him before he slept, "Jett? Did I hear you tell me you loved me?"

His eyes flew open and he stopped the gasp that would've come naturally. His mumblings while he was reviving her. He hadn't even thought about what he was saying; he was just letting his brain run freestyle. Had he said he loved her? And if he had, was it true?

One thing was sure. He wasn't ready to talk about it now. So, he faked a snore, which he hoped would buy him time till at least tomorrow.

Chapter Thirteen

Sadie had no idea how long she'd slept, but when she awoke, the sun was out, and Jett's bunk was empty.

She stretched her arms above her head and grimaced at an ache on her side. Nothing serious. Nothing she couldn't live with. But if she had her guess, she sported a shark-sized bruise where she'd gotten side-swiped.

She took advantage of the quiet time to take a shower, then dressed and headed above deck. She looked around for Jett, and when she couldn't find him, panic streaked through her. He wasn't below deck; he wasn't above deck. There weren't too many other places to be on a boat.

The sound of streaming water caught her attention on the port side. She walked to the ladder and watched Jett emerge from the ocean. When he was safely standing beside her, she punched him in the shoulder.

"Ow," he said.

"Are you crazy? Need I remind you, there's a shark down there!"

He held his hands up. "Whoa, whoa. No worries. He's moved on. I had to check the damage to the hull and decide if the yacht is seaworthy."

She stared, then said, "Well? How does it look?"

He smiled and stuck his thumb up in the air. "It actually looks pretty good. You did a good job down there in the limited time you had."

Relief poured through her. "So, you think we can race?"

"Yep. Ready to set sail?"

Inexplicable happiness filled her soul. She grabbed his shoulders and pulled him in for a kiss on the cheek. "Aye aye, Captain."

Jett raised the anchor, then they took their positions. At Jett's command, they started up the motor, and went through the steps to raise the sails and move into the wind. Before long, they were making good speed, with Jett carefully tracking the route and avoiding known problems in their way.

The sun sent strong beams from the sky and they worked together to operate the yacht. Despite the life-threatening problems they'd experienced during the night, Sadie knew she was developing the yacht sailing bug. Maybe when the race was over, she could go sailing with Jett and learn more techniques, more strategy. This was an expensive sport, and one requiring lots of knowledge. But maybe he could continue to teach her.

While they sailed, watching the winds, the sails, the position of the ship and the speed they were going, they passed the hours by talking. Sadie found him very easygoing, a great listener. And of course, easy on the eyes.

"How do you think your dad is doing?" Sadie asked during the mid-afternoon. The wind was pushing them solidly forward, and other than a few tack commands to take best advantage of the wind direction, their day of sailing had been smooth.

Jett released a scoff. "I have no idea."

"And you don't care," she finished for him.

"Absolutely."

Sadie presumed that his dad hadn't experienced the delay that they had, and therefore, was ahead of them in the race. "Do you assume he's ahead of us?"

Jett shrugged. "Until we get closer to the finish, we really have no way of knowing how the others are doing. We can just control how well we're doing and hope that it's enough."

"Do the other teams stop for the night?"

"Sometimes. It's a four-day race with a two-person crew, so yeah, sometimes they have to stop and catch some z's."

"Just keep going till it's over, right?"

His casual smile complimented his wavy hair blowing in the breeze. He was the picture of a carefree beach boy. "Yeah, that's always been my approach. Don't give up. Do the best you can. You never know."

The wind blew at the loose braid she'd formed in her hair. She liked that approach. It could be applied to way more than sailing races. It was a great way to approach all things in life.

"You're pretty smart, you know that?" She glanced over at him with a grin.

He chuckled. "And you're pretty great." He left his spot on the starboard and came closer to her, sitting beside her at the helm. "Look, I don't think I apologized to you last night. But I want you to know that I'm really, *really* sorry. I put you in danger and I would never forgive myself if you'd gotten hurt. Here you were kind enough to help me, and I scared the bejeezus out of you. I'm really sorry."

She leaned closer to him, the scent of sunscreen coming off his bare shoulders. "Don't be ridiculous. You saved my life! You put yourself in danger to fight off a shark. I mean, seriously, who does that?"

"You wouldn't have needed saving if I hadn't put you down in the water."

She shrugged. "I wouldn't have been in the water if I hadn't damaged your yacht."

He let out a frustrated sound. "Would you please let me take responsibility for this and tell you how sorry I am?"

She shook her head and grabbed his hand. "No. I won't let you take this on yourself. You want to know why? We're a team. The minute I agreed to be your first mate, we became a team with the single-minded goal to sail this race. We may not win. We may not even place. But together, we're competing. We're both responsible for our actions and our decisions. I rely on you and you rely on me. We couldn't do it without the other."

As she spoke, his expression morphed into disbelief. Several moments of silence slipped by while her words sank in. He shook his head. "You're amazing, Sadie. I've never met anyone like you. Ever."

She should've chuckled to lighten the moment, but a memory from the night before came to her mind. She had to know if what she thought she heard was true. Or had she imagined it, subliminally hoping it to be true? "Jett, last night, after you saved me from the shark, and I fainted, and you carried me above board and you were reviving me ..."

He took a breath to steel himself and moved his eyes away from hers.

"Did you tell me you loved me?"

At that moment she knew it was true. Not because of what he said, but because of what he didn't say. He didn't immediately deny it. He didn't laugh like she was crazy or accuse her of dreaming it up. The words floated between them while he prepared himself to answer honestly.

"I think I did."

It was her turn to chuckle. "You think you did?"

"Okay, I did. While I was reviving you, I was terrified that something was wrong, and you were in trouble. I couldn't imagine losing you and while I was bringing you back, that sentiment slipped out."

That sentiment. His love for her. Not guilt or regret that he'd put her in the water to be attacked by a shark. But the sentiment that slipped out while he was busy reviving her was his love for her. His heart must've known before his brain knew, because it just slipped out.

That meant it must be true. She needed to hear him say it, to confirm it. Or, at the very least, she needed him to accept it, to not deny it.

"I didn't think you would hear it." He looked away, still connected by their hands, and then he turned back, and his big happy smile wiped the breath from her lungs. "But I'm glad you did."

"You are?" she said breathlessly.

"Look, Sadie. I've been with a lot of women, but I've never had strong feelings for any of them, the feelings I had when I was looking at you, lying unconscious on the deck. I've always enjoyed women, but I've never loved one. But you. You're different than all of them. I've never met anyone like you."

She blinked. She didn't want to sound like an idiot, but she had to clarify. "Maybe you just felt protective, like I was your sister or something?"

He let loose a rush of laughter, his head tilting back to the sky. "I may never have been in love, but I'm pretty sure that what I feel for you is *not* what I would feel for a sister." He grabbed her shoulders and pulled her in for a kiss, as if to prove his point. Her heart raced at the mere contact of his lips on hers, but as they kissed, the depth of her feelings for him became more and more clear. Their relationship had grown from a working partnership to a love between two adults. It was completely new to her. She was on new ground because like him, she had never fallen in love before.

Unlike him, she had never even dated before.

They parted, but she stayed close. Honesty. He had been honest with her, and she need to return the honesty. She had no idea if she loved him, but she definitely had feelings for him. She needed to let him know. "I have feelings for you, too."

He smiled and rubbed his cheek against hers, caressing the back of her neck.

But she had more to say. "You say you've dated a lot of women. Well, I'm the opposite. I've never dated anyone."

He gave her a look of disbelief. "What? That can't be true. You're beautiful! You're smart and fun. How could any guy not see that?"

She shook her head. "I didn't say no one had ever asked me out on a date. I just never accepted. My view of love was formed by my parents' marriage. They both wanted different things in life, but bound to each other, neither one got what they wanted." She looked deep into his eyes to make sure he understood the gravity of her stance. "I don't want that for myself. I have goals in life. I don't want to have to give all that up because of love."

He sat quietly, then said, "Your parents' story is tragic for all three of you. But love doesn't always turn out that way. I hope that's an exception. In fact, I know it is." He cleared his throat and shifted to face her. "I would never want the woman I love to give up anything in life. I would be supportive of her goals and stand behind her and help her however I could."

It sounded good, it sounded perfect. But he was new to love too. He'd just admitted it.

"As far as you and I go, I'm going to throw this out on the table. Shoot it up if you want. I can take it." He grinned. "How about we move slowly in our relationship, so we can figure out if we are, indeed, right for each other?"

She blinked. This man was unbelievable. She didn't realize a man like him existed on this earth. Was he being truthful? Or just saying what he thought she wanted to hear? "Are you serious?"

"Serious as a shark attack."

She laughed. "Let's take this slow. Let's enjoy being together and getting to know each other before we declare a lifetime of love."

"See, I told you you were smart. That's a great plan." He pulled her in for another kiss, then pointed to the sails which were not taking full advantage of the wind. "Time to tack."

They both got to their feet and took positions.

"Ready to tack," Jett shouted.

"Ready to tack," Sadie responded.

And she got to work.

~ * ~

As the night approached, Sadie's nerves began to get the best of her. Sailing during the day when they were both awake was one thing. Jett was in charge and she carried out his orders under his watchful eye. But night time was when they split shifts. One grabbed sleep while the other sailed the ship alone. Nighttime was when she'd run the yacht aground a coral reef. Nighttime was when she'd encountered a shark in the water.

But she refused to let her fear overtake her. She had always prided herself on being fearless, daredevil, thrill-seeking. She could do this.

As the hours went by, and the sky darkened, her anxiety over the thought of commanding the yacht solo, increased. Until a few words from Jett released her fear.

"Let's stop from midnight to four am. I'll anchor the boat and we'll both catch sleep."

It was exactly what she wanted to hear, and yet she didn't. "Why?" she asked sharply. She refused to be babied; she needed to contribute as a fully functioning team member. Providing another reason to lose valuable time, to losing the race and the Sailtone contract, would be devastating to her.

He shrugged. "We both need the rest. Let's do what's right for our bodies and we'll finish strong tomorrow afternoon."

She clamped her mouth shut and watched him move toward the anchor. She should leave well enough alone, but she couldn't. She had to know. She followed him as he bent over the anchor, preparing to lower it. "Do you think I can't operate the yacht by myself? Do you think I'll go off course again?" She didn't mean her tone to be accusatory, but even to her own ears, it sounded that way.

Jett stopped what he was doing, turned to her and took her into his arms. "No! I don't think that at all. I just think we both need the rest. We've had a heck of a day. We've made great time. We've earned a few hours of sleep."

She rested her head against his chest. His steady, solid heartbeat gave her comfort. His heart was steady, and Jett was a steady guy. She didn't need to be suspicious of his motives or his actions. He only wanted what was best for the two of them, their team of two.

He wasn't like her mother, and she needed to give him the benefit of the doubt, take him at face value.

Jett was more like her father.

The realization pulled her head up and she studied his face. The stiffness in her shoulders softened. He had many of her father's positive attributes: ambitious, hard-working, goal-oriented. In fact, he was a lot like her. "Okay, sorry. I didn't mean to accuse you of anything."

He kissed her cheek. "No problem." He went back to his work with the anchor, and soon they were secured for the night.

Chapter Fourteen

At four o'clock Jett's phone alarm sounded. He jolted for a moment before his mind identified it. He had set the alarm. It was time to wake up.

He quieted the phone and laid back for a moment, his eyes closed. He breathed deeply in through his nose and his lips curled into a smile. He could smell Sadie across the cabin, and she smelled great. Her hair smelled of lemon, and her skin carried more of a coconut scent. The combination became uniquely her scent.

He glanced around the dark cabin and knew they needed to get up. It was time to finish the race today. According to his best calculations before he anchored, they were in pretty good position. Despite the accident and the time spent patching the hull, if they made good time today, their time was consistent with other races he'd done. No need to give up hope of a placement yet.

The thought would normally have him racing to his feet, but right now, he had something else on his mind. Sadie and her phenomenal scent and her luscious fit body lay just feet away in the dark, sleepy and warm. How he'd love to join her in her bunk, take her in his arms and show her just how strong his feelings were for her.

But he wouldn't. Sadie wasn't just any girl, she was the girl he'd fallen in love with. His feelings were different, and his approach would be different too. He wanted to fully get to know her; her hopes and dreams, her goals, her strengths and weaknesses; before he complicated things with physical intimacy. Not to mention, Sadie was a Christian; that much she'd made clear. And he respected that. He wanted to learn more about it from her, and he wanted to know how he could bring Christ more fully into his own life. Let God lead his actions and words.

So, pulling on a self-control he didn't even know he had, he dragged himself out of bed, crept over to her bunk and tapped her on the shoulder. "Time to get up, first mate."

She awoke immediately. "Okay, give me two minutes."

"Yep."

On deck a little later, they took a moment to eat protein bars for breakfast, then got to work.

"I'd like to check that patch job and make sure it's set for the day," he said. Her mouth dropped open and she went still. "No sharks," he said with a chuckle.

"You can't guarantee that!"

"I know. I'll do a quick up and down, one breath, two at the most." He located his diver's mask and put it on.

"I'm coming with you." She stood and planted her feet, as if she expected an argument. Instead, he picked up another diver's face mask and tossed it to her. She caught it with both hands.

"Okay. You stay at the ladder and watch out for beasties."

She let out a laugh. They made sure their masks fitted properly and he led Sadie through a few deep breathing exercises. He set the ladder in place, and they descended, Jett first. He grabbed a breath before going under water, and when he kicked off from the ladder, he turned to look behind him. Sadie was there on the bottom rung, giving him a thumbs up.

He swam quickly to the patched spot, wanting to do his examination on a single lungful of air. He fingered the length and width of the patch. It was holding, but he sure wished he had more putty. Twenty-four hours of speeding through the ocean had taken its toll on the patch, especially when Sadie'd had to abandon it before she was fully done. But he'd searched the yacht, all its nooks and crannies, for more putty this morning and couldn't find any.

He adjusted the putty already on the hole and hoped it would be enough.

He made his way back to the ladder. Sadie let him go up ahead of her. On deck, they both took off their masks and grabbed air into their lungs.

"So, what do you think, Captain?"

What good would it do to share his concerns that the putty wouldn't last the day? There was absolutely nothing they could do about it. Well, maybe one thing.

"Remember what you said about praying to God about little things, as well as big things?"

She nodded, her eyes focused on his.

"Would you say a prayer with me that the putty holds through the finish line?"

With those words, she understood exactly what he was saying. No other explanation was needed. She took his hands in hers, bowed her head and spoke into the broad open expanse of sea, "Dear Lord, creator of the sea and the earth, the heavens and all there is. We ask you to watch over Jett and me today and help us get safely over the finish line. Keep our boat dry and safe. In Jesus' name we pray. Amen."

"Amen," Jett murmured and looked up at her. "Short and sweet."

She smiled. "That's all it takes."

They got to work and soon they set sail. By ten in the morning, other boats dotted the horizon. All competitors were racing for the same ending point, so traffic was now becoming a reality, just like with the other open seas races he'd competed in. He pointed to a boat about a hundred yards away. Sadie followed his gesture and her face soon beamed a breathtaking smile of happiness.

"Getting close now," she shouted.

He nodded. Leaving her alone with the controls, he went below deck and studied his navigational software. Spending a few minutes alone with his thoughts, he came up with an advantageous route to the finish line, and then a Plan B in case it was needed.

The final hours of the race passed quickly, and Jett was fully aware of his adrenaline pumping wildly through his veins. They were in good shape; just how good, he didn't know.

They repositioned the boat and they were racing solidly when two more boats appeared in their line of sight. One of them caused a feeling of nausea in his stomach. "There he is."

"What?" Sadie glanced up and around.

"My dad's boat." He pointed to one of the yachts now within eye-shot. "The Wolverine. I could tell you how much he paid for that thing, and you would think he was nuts."

She gazed at it for a few moments and then said, "Well. How's he gonna feel when your hand-me-down boat and your novice first mate beat his butt in this race?"

He looked over at her, a smile forming. Her competitive spirit had emerged, just like his. They were cut from the same cloth, the two of them. It was one of the reasons he was so drawn to her. They were a perfect match.

He held out a fist and she pounded it with hers.

"What's our plan, Captain? We've gotten this far, now we've got to finish this thing. Give me some orders so I can help you get ahead of all these boats."

The last two hours of the race proved to be a test for his skills. With so much riding on the race results, his competitiveness charged into overdrive. Full throttle, they drove The Majestic through the waves, he and Sadie in sync with a common goal. He climbed to the top of the mast, overseeing the race and all the boats as they all pounded toward the finish line. He shouted down orders to Sadie, and she responded quickly and accurately, no hesitation from either of them. No caution now, just full speed ahead, giving it all they had.

Heart pounding, Jett directed Sadie to move the boat toward the port side. Closer to The Wolverine. He wanted to get close enough to see his father's face. Observe his reaction as Jett sailed ahead of him over the finish line.

The moment was almost here. The moment he'd been training for most of his life. Never before had he raced with this much on the line. Competing against his father, neck and neck toward the finish. He knew he could do it, if all went well, if he made good decisions and didn't go conservative. He had to put it all on the line.

"Jett! Jett!" Sadie's shouted voice came to him from below. "I hear splashing. I mean, water in the cabin."

He immediately climbed down from the mast. Sadie held firmly onto the helm, keeping them on course but she pointed to the stairwell. He scrambled down the stairs.

Water squirted wildly in from the port side of the hull. An inch of sea water covered about two-square-feet of the cabin floor. He sprang into action. He rummaged through the drawers until he found duct tape and plastic. The putty had evidently come loose on the exterior of the hull, but he needed to do what he could to stop the cabin from taking on more water. On his knees, he slid to the spot where water was entering. It wasn't a pour; maybe he'd caught it in time. He'd do a thorough job of patching the hull when the race was over but for now, he needed the boat to stay dry until he finished.

"Come on, baby," he murmured as he made quick work of filling the hole with a cloth and taping plastic over the whole spot. He observed for a solid five minutes as the boat continued to dash through the waves. The cotton he'd stuck in the hole had gotten soaked, but the water hadn't penetrated through the plastic. Maybe he'd caught a break.

He wiped up the standing water on the floor, and with one last glance, he joined Sadie on deck. "I did the best I could. We need to keep moving."

She gave him a devastated expression. "Is it flooding?"

He glanced at her. "A little bit. But I may have patched it enough to keep us alive."

Tears welled in her eyes and her forehead creased. He knew she felt guilty for damaging the hull, but as she said, they were team. They were in this together. "Hey, none of that. We're still in this race."

She cleared her throat. "Yep. Still in the race. Keep trying till it's over."

"Do your best." He smiled, and they kept racing.

~ * ~

Everything was happening so fast now. All she could do was to watch Jett, listen to his commands and follow them as best she could. Her heart raced when she watched him, his steady gaze at the sea, his easy movement around the big boat, his strong voice with solid confidence. This is what an expert in sailing looked like, sounded like. He had the heart of a champion and she was thrilled to be by his side.

She just hoped beyond hope that her error hadn't cost him the race of a lifetime. Because she'd never, ever be able to forgive herself if she had. If they lost the race because of flooding, she could forget about a relationship with the man.

Even if he told her it didn't matter, she knew it did.

Even if he tried to convince himself that the two of them had a future, she knew they were doomed.

The only way she could ever enter a relationship with Jett and explore their budding love for each other, was if she was on equal footing with him. She couldn't be the dummy who'd run the boat over a reef and tore it open, her blunder causing them to lose the race.

"Sadie!" Jett's voice came from up above. He was perched halfway up the mast, standing on a ladder rung. "I can see the finish line!"

She looked up at him, then followed his pointing finger. She tried to look but couldn't see from her angle. "Aye aye, Captain!" she shouted with an excited smile.

"Ready to jibe," he shouted.

"Ready to jibe," she responded and moved into position.

"Jibing!" They yelled in unison and she used her biceps to operate the winch, moving the sails in the direction the captain ordered. Still speeding ahead, they crashed through the waves. Jett stayed in position. They had almost caught up with The Wolverine, about fifty yards away on their starboard. She glanced at Jett. He must be happy with their progress. Two boats were placed in front; The Wolverine, and The Majestic were neck and neck. The two Martin captains vied for the bronze medal position.

Jett let out a whoop from his perch, a happy, hopeful sound that warmed her heart. She gripped the helm firmly, making sure the boat stayed true to the position Jett had set for it.

With the race close enough to the shoreline to hear the enthusiastic shouts and cheers of the spectators, and see the people waving colorful flags in the air, The Wolverine pulled ahead of The Majestic.

Just a yard at first. Sadie darted a look at Jett. What would he order? What command would he pull out of his captain's bag of tricks to catch up to their nemesis?

Another yard lengthened the distance between the two boats. "Jett!" she screamed. She didn't know what to do, but surely, he did.

A movement onboard The Wolverine drew her gaze in that crew's direction. Jett's dad leaned over the side of his boat, making gestures, screaming words she couldn't hear. But she could imagine them. Piecing together the clues: the distance between the two boats lengthening, Jett's father's derogatory gestures and haughty expression, accompanied by Jett's face.

His expression had darkened, his face had shut down. The finish line was approaching, but he knew he was defeated.

The Wolverine finished in third place, and The Majestic limped over the line in fourth.

Jett climbed off the mast and took over the helm. His hand brushed over hers and he leaned to start the motor. The race was over and although they'd finished, they hadn't placed in the top three. The Sailtone contract was lost, and to add insult to injury, he hadn't beaten his father.

"I'll take over to steer into the slip. You stand by, okay? We'll need to furl the sails."

She nodded, stunned, in a daze. They had held out hope for four days, and within minutes, all hopes were dashed. She watched Jett work, putting his expertise in action, performing all the intricate moves that she wouldn't have been able to do without him. But she couldn't help wondering, *What happened?*

Why were they overtaking The Wolverine one minute, and suddenly the other boat darted ahead? What had Jett's father done, that Jett hadn't done?

A splashing sound below was her answer. She turned to the stairway to below deck, walked down two steps and saw. The cabin was filled with water. "Jett!" she screamed. "We're flooded!"

He nodded. "I figured. We'll take care of it. Let me just get to the slip."

She gazed down the steps. Every object that wasn't secured was floating in at least two feet of water. The entire lower cabin of the boat was a swimming pool.

No wonder The Majestic couldn't sail as fast as The Wolverine in the last few moments of the race. It was toting gallons and gallons of extra seawater.

Chapter Fifteen

Jett kept busy after crossing the finish line. There was always a lot of tasks to do, and since they didn't place in the top three, there was no reason to hang around and drink champagne. He maneuvered the boat to its temporary slip and instructed Sadie on lowering the sails and getting them secured. He'd need to identify the right race officials to help him with re-patching the hull. He had to decide whether to get the hull repaired here in Bermuda so they could sail it home, or arrange to get the boat transported back to Murrells Inlet. But first they'd need to bail out this water.

He and Sadie worked quietly and efficiently together. His disappointment over the results prevented him from chatting happily with her, but she knew how he felt. She was as much a competitor as he was, if not more. There was no reason to celebrate. They hadn't reached their goals.

On the other hand, they were both safe, they'd finished the race, and except for a hole in his boat, The Majestic was intact too. There would be other races. Once he was physically recovered, he'd go back to his real event, sailing single-handed.

Then a different thought crept into his mind. He and Sadie made a good team, despite the accident. They thought alike; they were in sync. If they were able to finish fourth in a premiere race while he had a broken rib, just think what they could do in a double-handed race if he were healthy. A bubble of excitement rose in his throat when he thought about competing in the sport he loved with the woman he loved. The dream brought him a few seconds of optimism in an otherwise gloomy day.

Grabbing buckets, Sadie and Jett went below deck and removed seawater from the cabin—the water that had lost them the race. Filling buckets down below, they climbed the stairs, dumped the water over and returned down below. Keeping busy kept Jett's mind away from the crushing results of the day, gave him a purpose, kept him from plunging into sadness.

"Too bad, so sad, bucko."

The voice, as well as the words, grabbed his heart and twisted. He'd recognize that voice anywhere. He'd been raised with it. He'd spent way too many days of his first eighteen years or so, surrounded by it. Wrapped up in it. Infuriated by it. That voice had cemented his decision to make a future for himself completely different than what was planned for him.

He directed a grim expression to Sadie. "I need to go up there and face him. I strongly urge you to stay down here."

She grimaced. "No. I'm coming with you."

He studied her face for a moment, then nodded his agreement. Holding out a hand, he gripped hers and led her to the stairs.

His father stood on the pier, a celebratory smile covering his face. The man had no idea how to show empathy and never had. "Hello, Dad."

Sadie made a sound next to him, and he looked at her. He realized in his attempt to deal with his father, he was squeezing her hand much more tightly than he intended. He dropped her hand, and she shook it out. They shared a sad smile. He whispered, "Sorry."

"What do you have going on there?" his father asked, pointing to their buckets.

"Damage to the hull. We patched it during the race, but it gave way in the last stretch."

His father's expression flickered with a mixture of emotions. Jett could read it like a book. He was elated that Jett and Sadie had lost the race, but he quickly transitioned to embarrassment. If his son, the ne'er do well, had come that close to beating him with a hole in his boat, he most certainly would've beat him without the damage.

Jett let that set for a while in his dad's psyche. To stick a nail in further, Jett asked calmly, "How about you? Did your yacht sustain any damage?"

As expected, his father hesitated before answering. If he admitted that his race had gone smoothly, it was a suggestion that Jett was the superior sailor.

"No," he responded finally. "The best sailors don't put holes in their boats, do they, son?"

His answer was so predictable, so supremely Cameron Martin, that Jett spit out a chortle. He was about to respond, to humor him, to agree with his assertion just to keep peace so they could move on, when Sadie spoke up. "You're absolutely right, Mr. Martin. Jett is an expert sailor. He would never put a hole in his boat. It was me. I was sailing when the damage happened."

Jett's heart filled with admiration for her. Her brave admission opened her to just as much danger as she'd faced down in the dark ocean with a shark patrolling around. His father could take those words and rip her apart easily. He'd done it to Jett countless times. It was why Jett had erased him completely out of his life as early as was possible.

But now dear old Dad was faced with a dilemma. As much as he yearned to maximize this opportunity to berate and humiliate, he had certain boundaries. He wouldn't willingly destroy a female. It was one of the only honorable things he'd ever witnessed in his father. Bemused, Jett watched his father's mind turn as he figured out how to work his way out of this one.

"Young lady, my son put you in a precarious position. You're inexperienced in the sport of sailing, and he put his own needs ahead of yours. He had no business putting you in charge of the yacht, and now you're paying the price for his bad judgement."

Jett's heart had hardened years ago, due to extended exposure to his father's spewed hate. He suspected his father would find a way to twist Sadie's words to be Jett's fault. He didn't need her to defend him and didn't expect her next comment.

"You should be ashamed of yourself, Mr. Martin. You have a remarkable son. Strong and courageous and ambitious as they come. But all you've ever taught him is that he didn't hit the mark. That he was a disappointment. That he didn't live up to your expectations of him. You could've easily destroyed a child with less character, but all you did was make Jett more determined to live his life on his own terms. As far as I'm concerned, you completely wasted your only opportunity at fatherhood."

During her speech, Jett's astonishment grew. His jaw dropped open, his eyes widened. No one had ever stuck up for him like this, and he couldn't imagine that it would ever be repeated in the future. His hands shook, and he turned to Sadie, basking in the glory of her reprimand of the one man who had most impacted his life.

In that moment, he knew he'd found the one woman he wanted to share the rest of his life with. His soulmate. His partner in everything.

Sweeping his gaze back to his father as she finished, he almost laughed. He was quite sure no one had ever spoken to him that way and he had no idea how to respond. But he reacted in kind, pulling up the negativity that colored everything else in his life.

"Young lady, you have no right to speak to me that way. You have no idea what it was like to parent this young man, and what he put me and his mother through. I will thank you to keep your invalid thoughts to yourself."

"Dad," Jett said, "it's time for you to leave. Congratulations on your bronze medal, but Sadie and I have work to do."

With that, he grabbed Sadie's hand and they returned down the stairs to the soggy cabin. Her shoulders shook, and he recognized the pent-up anger in her, wanting to escape. His father had caused that same need in himself, many times. But he didn't want to give his dad the satisfaction of knowing that he'd caused them anger. In his father's mind, that would be another checkmark in the win column. Instead, he pulled Sadie into his arms and held her tight. He absorbed her body's shudders into his own, and took her anger as his own. They were a team. He could help her with this. For her, it was new, but he'd been dealing with it his entire life.

She quieted and finally he pulled away, holding onto her shoulders so he could see her face. "Thank you for standing up for me."

She let out a scoff. "It was nothing. It was the least I could do. Unfortunately, he didn't get it. Nothing will change for you."

He shook his head. "You don't understand. It wasn't nothing, it was huge. It was unbelievable. No one has ever stood up for me against my father's abuse. Never."

She frowned. "Not even your mother?"

"Especially not my mother. My dear mother's way of dealing with her husband is to avoid conflict. Whatever he did, whatever he said, she swept it under the rug. 'It's okay,' she'd say. 'You're okay.' But she never saw that I wasn't okay. You did, Sadie. You did."

He cradled her head in his hands, sweeping her hair up as he brought his lips to rest on hers. His heart pounded as they kissed, as her lips tangled with his, equals in passion. Despite the horribleness of this day, despite the failure and disappointment, it was the best day of his life. He'd found, with no uncertainty, someone he didn't even know he was looking for. He'd found his Sadie.

He pulled away and placed his forehead on hers. "I love you, Sadie."

Her eyes went wide, and she caught her breath. Her shaking started again, this time in her hands. An uncomfortable moment passed, and she pulled back from him, one step, two.

"Hey, Jett," she said in an awkward cadence. "Can you handle this without me? I feel like I need to call some classmates and get caught up on the schoolwork I missed."

He blinked. Schoolwork? Now? He caught his breath. She was trying to escape him, of that he was sure. He had no idea why. "Yeah, sure. Yep. I need to bail this water out, then get the hole patched. Sure."

She turned and took a step away.

"Catch up with you for dinner?"

She paused but didn't respond. He watched her jog away.

~ * ~

Sadie forced herself not to look back. She put as much distance between her and Jett as she could, as fast as possible.

He loved her, and she thought she loved him too. But she couldn't stay with him now. Not when she'd damaged his boat, lost him the race and the Sailtone contract, and given his father one more reason to berate and criticize him.

Even she, who had no experience with relationships, knew that starting a life with someone on top of that rocky foundation, was a disaster waiting to happen.

Sure, she thought as she raced to a nearby coffee shop, he said he loved her. Today. But when he really started thinking of the mistake she'd made, and how much it cost him, he not only wouldn't love her. He would hate her. He would resent her. How could she blame him? She'd made a total mess out of their racing partnership. Although she could walk away scot-free, he would have to face the consequences of her actions.

Inside, she sat at a table and used her phone to book a flight to Myrtle Beach. Today. If she stuck around and spent more than one more minute with Jett Martin, she may not have the will to do what she knew she had to do, for both of them.

~ * ~

His work was done, at least for today. He'd finished bailing out the cabin, wiped all the surfaces dry and contacted a company to do the permanent repair on his hull. He'd supervise them tomorrow, delaying his return sail to the South Carolina coast. He now had two full days to spend with the woman he loved on the charming island of Bermuda.

He walked into downtown St. George, one of the two main towns on the island. He'd been here before, although never with The Majestic. Bermuda was a British island with a rich history, charming architecture and stunning beaches. He could think of no better place to continue to get to know the amazing woman he'd fallen in love with.

But first, he needed to locate her. He'd sent her several texts with no reply. He'd called her as well. Either cell service wasn't working for their phones in Bermuda, or she was purposely avoiding him.

That second possibility caused a feeling like a knife to his gut.

He walked along the sidewalk in front of some pastel-painted buildings, the sun shining on him bright and warm, and yet his mind was in a dark place. Where was she? Why had she left him so suddenly?

From his shorts pocket, his phone rang. He pulled it out and his heart leaped. "Sadie! Thank God! I was starting to get worried about you."

"Sorry about that, Jett. I didn't mean to make you worry."

He smiled at the sound of her voice. "No problem. Where are you? I thought we could spend some time together on the island until the hull is repaired."

"Oh, um, I'm sorry, Jett," she began, and his heart plunged.

"What? What are you sorry about?"

"I have to get home. I bought a flight and actually, I need to take a cab to the airport soon."

His head started to spin. She was leaving? "Wait. Where are you? Let's talk about this before you go."

"Jett," she said, and her voice faltered. She sniffed, and he knew she was starting to cry. "I can't tell you how sorry I am. I caused all this bad stuff to happen to you, and you don't deserve that."

He paused, his head trying to catch up with her words. "What? What bad stuff? Sadie, let me see you. Let's talk this out."

"I – I've got to go, Jett. I want to thank you for believing in me. But I think it's best if we don't see each other anymore."

His heart rate spiked. "No! No, Sadie."

Her next words, "I'm sorry," were a whisper he could barely hear before the line went dead.

Chapter Sixteen

Slipping back into her post-yacht race routine was proving difficult for Sadie. Her failure as Jett's first mate weighed heavily on her conscience and it soon permeated her confidence in other areas of her life.

She stared at herself in the bathroom mirror, attempting to apply mascara. Instead of concentrating on the task, her mind ran. She wasn't used to failure. A hard worker at everything in her life, she never accepted defeat. Sure, she was learning to be a successful marathon runner. But what made her think she could try to master other extreme sports, if her first try had ended up in failure?

She capped the wand, satisfied with an incomplete job, glad she hadn't stabbed her eye in the process. She made her way to the kitchen. She pulled two hard boiled eggs and a yogurt from the refrigerator and sat at the table to eat.

Her dad walked in, poured himself a cup of coffee from the pot already brewed, and set it on the table. He popped two pieces of bread in the toaster and studied her while he waited. "Busy day today?"

She shrugged without looking up. "Class."

He paused. "You going to the gym?"

"No," she said, then shook her head. "I quit going there."

He slid into a chair opposite her with his toast. "Really? I thought you enjoyed going there."

She looked up at him, then back down at her breakfast. "I know what I'm doing with my marathon training. I can do it without going to the gym."

She finished her first egg and concentrated on peeling the second one. Her dad lowered his mug to the table with a loud thud, the hot liquid splashing over the side. She looked up at him with a surprised glance.

"Dang it, Sadie, what's going on with you? I've never seen you this down. Something happened on that boat race, I'm sure of it, and I want to know what it is."

She studied his face, her mind whirring. She'd been closed-mouthed about her feelings for Jett. Her dad had no idea what had transpired during those days at sea. Maybe it was time to share a little bit. Maybe he could help. Her dad had never let her down before.

"Okay. Yes, something did happen during the race. I messed up."

Dad shook his head, a frown on his lips. "You said you guys placed fourth. That sounds like a great placement in such a big race."

"Fourth may as well be last, under the circumstances." Dang tears threatened in her eyes. She took a knuckle and wiped them roughly. She'd cried enough tears over the last few days, she should be done by now. She drew in a deep breath. "I told you about Jett's invention?"

Her dad nodded.

"The agreement was that he'd get the contract from Sailtone if he placed in the top three."

Her dad lifted a shoulder. "Okay, so he missed the contract. There will be other chances. How is this your fault, Sadie-girl?"

"I damaged his boat, Dad. I ran it atop a coral reef and put a hole in the bottom of it. We patched it, but it didn't hold. By the time we approached the finish line, the cabin was flooding." She couldn't prevent the sob that escaped from her mouth.

He reached across the table and placed his big warm hand over hers. "I'm sure it wasn't just your fault. Where was Jett?"

"No, it was my fault entirely. He trusted me to take a shift while he slept. And I blew it. I sailed his big beautiful yacht over a reef and ripped a hole in it. I'm the reason we lost, Dad. I'm the reason he lost the contract."

Tears flowed openly now, and she didn't even try to wipe them away. Dad handed her a napkin and pulled the chair over beside hers. He wrapped an arm around her shoulders and held her tight. He gave her the time to cry, to let it out.

When she was done, he said, "It was an accident, honey. You didn't do it on purpose."

"Of course, I didn't do it on purpose, but I still did it. I can't forgive myself. And I certainly can't face him. He's so much better off without seeing me as a constant reminder."

Her dad patted her shoulder, much like he had throughout her childhood when she'd limped home with a scraped knee from skateboarding, roller skating or bike riding. "Is that why you quit going to the gym?" he asked quietly. "Because you don't want to face him?"

Her admission was painful, shameful. She nodded.

He turned to her. "Is he making you feel bad about this?"

"No! Just the opposite. He keeps saying it was his fault that he put me in a position to fail." She held her tongue. What she'd said was true, but she wasn't going to tell her dad that Jett had confessed his love for her as well. It would just confuse things further.

"I'm sorry about what happened. He's right that you didn't have very long to prepare for this race. But with your athleticism and smarts, he must've had confidence that you would be a valuable partner. Accidents happen, sweetheart. Tell you what. Why don't I offer him some funds to help pay for the repairs? Would that help you feel a little less guilty about it?"

She blinked, her face a stone wall. Funds? Oh Lord, she hadn't even thought about the expense she'd caused Jett to repair the boat. One more thing to worry about. "I don't know, Dad. Don't boats have insurance for damage?" She shook her head. "Let me think about it." Offering Jett her dad's money would mean another face-to-face meeting with him, and she didn't think she could do that. Not when her heart had imagined what life would be like right now if she hadn't messed up. She'd be Jett's girlfriend, dating him, seeing him all the time. Maybe she'd be madly in love with him by now.

No, she needed to be strong and keep her distance.

"Okay, you give me the word. I'd be happy to help. Now, on another topic." He stood and dragged his chair back in place while she got herself together. "Nora and I have picked a wedding date."

"You have?" A jolt of happiness went through her. Something happy. Just what she needed as a diversion from all the sadness.

"Yes, and it's quick. The weekend after next. Very simple ceremony in Nora's pasture, just cake, punch and cookies in the mansion afterward. We put together a guest list. Very small. We're thinking less than thirty people, total."

"That's awesome, Dad! I want to help with arrangements."

Shaw examined her face. "Are you sure you still want to? Don't you have enough on your mind?"

"Now more than ever. I need a fun project to focus on."

"I understand. Why don't you talk to Nora and see what still needs to be done?"

She pushed the remnants of her breakfast aside, stood and kissed him on the cheek. "I'll do that, Dad. I'm so happy for you." She grabbed her backpack and made her way to the door.

"Hang in there, sweetheart."

~ * ~

Jett checked his schedule at the gym and noticed he had a ninety-minute break before his next client. He could sit around here and let his mind churn like it had been since his return from Bermuda. An endless clip of disappointment and depression. Or he could keep busy.

"Hey," he said to the new receptionist behind the front desk. "I'm heading out. I'll be back in time for my next appointment."

She shot him a charming smile, accompanied with a shoulder tilt. "Sounds good, Jett. See you soon."

The girl had only been working at the gym for a week or so. He looked at her with new eyes. Maybe he should get friendly with her, ask her out, spend a little time with her. Maybe a distraction of the female variety would help him forget the one woman who absorbed his thoughts and his mood.

Sadie Flynn.

She dominated his mind; he couldn't stop thinking of her. Her rejection of him was complete and unbendable. She walked off his yacht, off the island, and out of his life without a glance back. After ten days of distance, he was still trying to piece together, why.

He knew she felt guilty about damaging his boat. Which indirectly ended up costing him a top three finish. But it wasn't her fault. He never should've put her in charge of the boat racing through the dark ocean in the middle of the night. What was he thinking? That one decision had derailed not only the race, but his budding relationship with the most perfect woman in the world.

In addition to her own guilt, was she also disappointed in him? In his inability to pull out a win after the accident? He was accustomed to not living up to people's expectations of him. That should be nothing new, however if that added to the complete absence of Sadie in his life, it hurt more than any of them.

He grabbed his wallet and keys and left the gym, heaving a deep sigh. He jumped into his truck and started driving. If he could just talk to her, see what was on her mind, try to change her mind, it would help. But she wasn't responding to his texts or calls. Even the ones where he begged her to talk to him, so they could work this thing out. He made it clear he was still interested in forming a relationship with her. But relationships were two-way streets, and in this one, she had put up a dead end.

He had no idea what to do. Take a hint and leave her alone? Let his heart heal and move on? That idea scraped his insides. But how could he continue to pursue her without seeming like a stalker? He needed help, he needed advice.

That's when it dawned on him. He'd approached this all wrong. He needed to put it in God's hands. He pulled the truck over into the next parking lot, bowed his head and prayed, "Dear Lord, I need your help. I've made a total mess of my relationship with Sadie. I think I'm in love with her but she's avoiding me, and I can't talk to her to find out what she's thinking. Please help me understand my next steps. Where would you guide me to go? Help me to find your will and help me to accept it. And Lord, don't hesitate to hit me over the head with it, because I'm new to this and I want to do it right." He sat in the silent vehicle, eyes closed, hands clasped, head bowed. His words had initiated a connection with his heavenly father. He felt it, and he didn't want it to end. He didn't know what else to say, but he knew that God already knew what was in his heart, and words weren't necessary. He concentrated on sending honest sentiments to God about his problem and hoped that he would receive a response. Some response. Not necessarily a booming voice out of the heavens. But something that he was sure about.

Minutes passed, and the strong connection eventually faded. "Amen," Jett said firmly and opened his eyes. He looked around, wondering if anything would be different now that he'd laid out his heart to God and asked for his help. Maybe it wouldn't happen this fast. Or maybe it wouldn't happen at all. But he had to stay hopeful. *Ask and you shall receive. Seek and you will find.* The Bible taught that. He needed to go with it.

He turned his head, looking at his surroundings. He had pulled into what looked like a small warehouse with corrugated metal walls. He steered his truck closer to the building and parked, turning off his engine. He read the sign, Coastline Pet Supply. He sat in the quiet of the truck for a moment, then turned the engine back on. God worked in his own time, Jett knew that. He could send a response this moment, next week, or next year. Jett had done his part by asking for help. Now, he needed to let God be God.

He shifted the truck into Reverse. The front door of the pet supply store opened, and a man wearing jeans, boots, cowboy hat and white button-down shirt walked out, carrying a large bag. Jett stared at the man. He looked familiar. He shifted the truck back into Park.

The cowboy carried the heavy bag of horse feed and swung it into the bed of his own pickup truck. Without analyzing, Jett opened the door and slid to his feet on the cement. "Excuse me," he said in the man's direction.

The cowboy looked in his direction. He stared for a moment, then a dawning of recognition flickered across the man's face. "You're Jett, aren't you?"

The minute he said it, the cowboy's identity became clear. "Dr. Flynn." He reached out for a handshake.

"Congratulations on your fourth-place finish in the race. Quite an accomplishment."

His words were kind and casual and as Jett looked at his face, he recognized the features that Dr. Flynn had passed on to his daughter. They had the same eye shape, the same cheekbones. "Thank you very much. It was quite a race, I'll say that."

An awkward moment of silence passed between them and Jett knew he had to dig deep within himself and speak about his concerns, his confusion. He was fully convinced that God had placed him here, in front of Sadie's father. He couldn't waste this divine intervention.

"Dr. Flynn, do you have a minute? I would love to talk to you about something."

Sadie's dad dipped his head, his lips forming into a small smile. "Sure." He gestured to his truck, opened the passenger side and walked around to the driver's seat. Jett climbed in. "You have something on your mind?"

"Yes." Jett cleared his throat and scarcely realizing it, he rubbed his hands together. "It's Sadie. She was a huge help to me, answering my call for help when I broke a rib and couldn't sail single-handed. She picked up the techniques of sailing with amazing speed. I thought we made a good team out there. And like you said, we placed strong. But ..." He ground to a halt because he had no idea how much to share. This was Sadie's father. Would she even want him sharing his feelings with her dad? Or would she tell him to leave her parent out of it?

He closed his eyes briefly and thought again, *Ask and you shall receive.* He was going to ask, he was going to share. Why not? He couldn't find himself in any worse shape than he was right now.

Turning back to Dr. Flynn, he let it out. "Sadie left me in Bermuda. We had plans to sail back together but she bought a plane ticket and flew home early. And I know she's busy, and I know she had to get back for school. But she isn't speaking to me, sir. She's ignored all my attempts to reach her and I just need to talk to her, to clear the air."

Sadie's father frowned. "Really? Well, that's not like her at all. I can't imagine why she'd leave you high and dry like that."

"I think I know. On the yacht, I told her I had developed feelings for her. I told her ... I loved her." He glanced down at his lap. "I'm in love with your daughter. And I've never felt this strongly for anyone. I have no idea what I'm doing."

His admission hung in the air, and to Jett, it seemed to crackle with electricity. Fortunately, Dr. Flynn finally spoke. "Are you mad at Sadie for damaging your yacht?"

Jett's head whipped in his direction. "No! Not at all. I made a bad judgement call when I put her in charge for a night shift. I realized too late that I was expecting way too much of her."

Dr. Flynn nodded. "Sadie catches on to things so quickly, it sometimes makes you forget she may not be ready. I've been there, done that myself. Son, this is new ground for me, because I haven't met many ... if any ... of Sadie's boyfriends. But I can tell you that she feels extremely guilty about causing that damage and she feels that it's her fault that you lost the race."

"I know. She told me. And that's one of the things I need to talk to her about. I can't allow her to take responsibility for that. That was my fault."

"Sounds like the two of you need to talk."

"Yes! I hate to ask, but can you help make that happen?"

Sadie's dad sat thoughtfully for a moment, then reached into the back seat and extracted a white box. He pulled off a lid. "I think I have an idea. You need to catch Sadie when she's happy and distracted. I have just the thing." He reached into the box and pulled out a card and handed it to Jett.

It was a photo of a smiling Dr. Flynn, an attractive woman and a black horse, surrounded by green grass. Words printed underneath the picture invited Jett to a wedding. A smile popped onto his face. "Your wedding?"

"Yeah, just picked those up from the printer. It's unusual, but it might just be the perfect place for you to talk. Surrounded by love."

Jett chuckled. "I hope you're right. I just hope she doesn't make a scene at your wedding."

Dr. Flynn shook his head. "She won't. She's worked too hard on planning it." The older man held a hand out and Jett took it. "I want Sadie to be happy. Maybe you're the one who can give her that."

Jett returned to his truck, his heart beaming. He'd received his message from God; he was sure of it.

Chapter Seventeen

The next few days after the divine meeting he was sure was planned by God, Jett's whole mood had changed. Gone was his depression, his feeling of hopelessness. Hope had been restored. He was going to see Sadie, and her father had suggested it. Had endorsed him. That had to carry weight with Sadie, since she loved her dad so much.

He was wrapping up for the day at the gym and was on his way out to the marina. He wanted to get some nautical miles on the repaired hull and ensure it was waterproof before racing The Majestic again. His phone rang. He grabbed it from the passenger seat and glanced at it. It was Mason, his Sailtone contact.

"Hey Mason."

"Buddy!" said Mason cheerfully. Jett held the phone out and looked at it. The last time he'd talked to Mason, he'd shared their fourth-place win and Mason didn't sound that cheerful.

"I've got some good news to share," Mason continued. "Drumroll?" He laughed cheerfully. "Manufacturing on your sunscreen product is approved. It's moving forward."

Jett's foot landed on the brake without any command from his brain. The truck screeched to a halt and Jett darted a look in the rearview mirror. A few cars behind him had to stop suddenly too, to avoid a collision. He eased the truck onto the shoulder and leaned back in his seat. "What did you say?"

"You're getting funded."

"But I didn't place in the top three of the Newport Bermuda race. I didn't hold up my end of the bargain."

Mason chuckled. "It's your lucky day. Fred Romine found some extra funding. He gave Margaret Foster, our head of Manufacturing, her choice on an additional project to kick off. She liked your demo and your passion. She picked yours."

Jett's heart pumped blood through his body, causing his hands to go a little shaky. "Are you serious? Are you joking with me right now?"

"I wouldn't do that to you, buddy. This is one hundred percent legit. They liked your product. They're going to produce it."

"Wow," Jett breathed.

"I'll pull the papers together. A contract, a compensation plan and a manufacturing schedule. From now on you'll be receiving regular quarterly paychecks from Sailtone. You're on the payroll, dude!"

Jett let out a laugh. This was unreal.

"Once we're closer to release, we want you to film some commercials, some promo. We'll also get some of the big-time boat shows on your calendar, so you can make personal appearances, endorsing the product."

"Yeah," was all he could get out of his mouth.

"Jett, mark this day on your calendar. This is the day your entire life changes. You've worked hard, and this is the day it pays off."

Mason continued to jabber but Jett couldn't remember too much of the content after he hung up. He was too focused on giving thanks and praise to the One who had supported him all along.

~ * ~

They say that rain is lucky for your wedding day. But Sadie was happy that her dad and his bride got a beautiful sunny Grand Strand day instead.

She was also happy that she'd taken on such a large role in throwing together this spontaneous wedding and reception. It had given her something to focus on and taken her mind off her first disastrous experience with love, brief as it may have been.

She put the finishing touches on her hair and makeup in the bathroom mirror and cleared her throat. Today was all about being happy. Her happiness for her father and Nora was over the top, and that was the only thing she would be thinking about today. That, and making this a day they would both remember forever.

She headed downstairs. Her dad stood in the kitchen, and at the sight of him, a smile burst onto her face. His plain dark suit accentuated his brown hair and tanned skin. The yellow tie provided a burst of color that, Sadie knew but her dad didn't yet, would match the daisies and yellow roses in Nora's bouquet. And because it was such a part of him, he also wore his cowboy hat.

She pulled him into her arms for a quick hug. "You look magnificent, Groom."

He shook his head. "I suppose all this is necessary. It seems a little fancy for a ceremony in a pasture with a horse."

Sadie laughed. "Hey, you're getting off easy. I could've planned a wedding fit for a prince and princess if I had the time and budget."

"I just want to marry her."

"And you will. Soon." She checked the digital clock on the microwave. "In fact, I need to leave and get over there. I have a few duties before the guests come." She stopped at the door. "You gonna be all right?"

"Never better."

"Okay, see you in one hour."

She headed off and drove over to Nora's property. She walked straight through her front door into the beautiful Georgian mansion that Nora had recently completed renovating. An inheritance from Nora's favorite aunt, it still took Sadie's breath away each time she set foot in here. "Nora?"

"Up here!"

Sadie climbed the grand center staircase, thinking of Scarlett O'Hara the whole way. Nora sat in a chair in her bedroom, in front of her vanity. A woman stood behind her with a curling iron.

"Sadie," Nora exclaimed. "Do you believe we're actually going to pull this off?"

Sadie swept in and placed a kiss on Nora's cheek. "You can do a lot of planning in ten days."

"We could've done it without you, but it wouldn't have been nearly this beautiful. Thank you again."

Sadie's cheeks warmed with the compliment.

"This is my sister, Patty. She has the distinction of being present the first moment I met your dad. Patty knew I loved him way before I realized it myself. Patty, this is Shaw's daughter, Sadie."

Patty put the curling iron down and approached Sadie, her hands out for a greeting. "Sadie, so nice to meet you in person. Nora's told me so much about you. You're lovely and you have such a wonderful dad."

The three women chatted and finished Nora's hair and finally the bride stood.

"Oh Nora," Sadie breathed. "You look gorgeous."

Nora had chosen a breezy, gauzy long dress in a shimmering champagne color. It skimmed over her slim body and was the picture of femininity. "You think?"

"I know," Sadie said with a smile. "Dad's going to love it."

Nora laughed nervously. Patty said, "I told her that too."

The next few hours flew by for Sadie. The wooden pagoda was delivered and placed in the center of the pasture. The florists brought massive vases of yellow and white flowers to decorate the pagoda and the guests' seating area. The rental company brought and set up thirty chairs in the pasture, leaving an aisle down the middle.

The cake arrived as well, and Sadie supervised the assembly of the multiple layers. She pulled out the cake topper she'd found, the bride and groom wearing cowboy hats, and then she pulled out a plastic child's toy, a black horse to join them on the top layer.

Sadie was arranging the serving table when Patty joined her. "Let me help you with the food. If there's one thing I'm good at, it's food."

Sadie laughed. "You've got a deal. How's Nora feeling?"

"Surprisingly, calm. This is what she wants, and she knows it."

The doorbell rang. Sadie opened it to find two teenaged boys from Oceanview Church she'd recruited to serve as parking attendants. "So glad you're here! Guests should be arriving any time." She led them off the porch and filled them in on where and how the guests should park.

Her dad pulled up in his truck and she waited to greet him. "No seeing the bride, you. You're going to the barn until it's time to meet under the pagoda."

He chuckled good-naturedly. "I remember. You've gone over all of this with us."

Pastor Ralph arrived, and she pointed out the pagoda where the wedding would take place. Things were really happening fast now, with the wedding time getting so close. A beautiful red-headed young woman emerged from the passenger side of a car. Or, she tried to emerge. Her driver, a good-looking young man jogged from the driver's side to help her. Once she was on her feet, Sadie saw why. The woman was in the late stages of pregnancy, judging from the size of her stomach. Sadie smiled and walked over to her.

"You must be Carly. I'm Sadie."

Carly smiled and made quick introductions. "Hi Sadie, so nice to meet you. This is my husband, Ryan and daughter, Grace."

Sadie bent to the cute little girl, a strawberry blonde dressed in an adorable red dress. "Hi Grace. Are you going to help your mama?"

"Yes! I'm going to hand out programs to the wedding guests."

Sadie laughed in delight.

"We've been practicing that for two days," Ryan said. "She's so excited to have a job, you'd think she was the bride." They all laughed. "Just point us in the right direction and we'll get to work."

Sadie nodded at Carly's bulging stomach. "Congratulations. When are you due?"

She puffed a labored breath. "Still a month away, if you can believe it. I'm already a house."

Ryan wrapped an arm around her shoulder. "I keep telling her she's the most beautiful pregnant woman in the world, but she insists on arguing with me."

Carly rolled her eyes, then put her hand on Sadie's arm. "I promise I won't give birth during the ceremony. Nora's been such a huge help to me, I wouldn't do that to her."

Sadie smiled. "You were one of her clients at Dress for Success, weren't you?"

"Her very first client. She helped me move from being a waitress to a college Admissions Rep, and guess what. I just got my first promotion. Couldn't have done it without her."

"She'll be so glad to see you."

They waved and moved on. Cars were streaming in now. Time was close. Sadie walked back to the house. Nora stood in the great room with Patty and Pastor Ralph.

"Oh Sadie, come join us. We were just going to pray with the pastor."

Sadie went to their circle and joined hands. Pastor Ralph prayed, "Lord, we thank you for love and especially today, for the love of this couple, Nora and Shaw. We ask that you watch over both of them today, as well as all their guests, and make this day a special oasis of love in the lives of all. Amen."

Sadie smiled. "A special oasis of love. I like that, Pastor."

Soon, the ceremony was underway. Pastor Ralph took his place under the pagoda, a Bible in his hands. Her father led Thunder, the big black gelding out to the pasture, releasing the halter and taking his place on the wooden platform. The horse, curious about all the activity in his field, stood behind the pagoda near Shaw. Guests had all found seats. A cello player sat to the right, serenading the guests with the haunting sound of a stringed melody.

Sadie gazed up, her face raised to the beautiful South Carolina sunshine and said her own silent prayer of thanks to God for giving this perfect day her father and the one he loved.

Her work was done, at least for now. She accepted a program from adorable Grace and located an empty seat on the groom's side. As she sat, her attention was drawn to someone seated two rows up. Was that ...? No, it couldn't be.

She peered, leaning forward to get a good view between guests' heads.

Yes! Jett Martin!

What was he doing here? How had he even known about the wedding?

Her pulse thudded through her veins. Standing up and leaving was an impossibility. Avoiding him after the short service would also be unlikely.

She would have to confront him after the service. She'd avoided him long enough. It was time to be honest.

Pastor Ralph began. "Friends and family, thank you for joining us on this beautiful day that our Lord has made. We are here to join together in holy matrimony, this man, Shaw Flynn, and this woman, Nora Ramsey. God has made it very clear to us how he feels about the institution of marriage. In fact, the apostle Paul's letter to the Corinthians contains a message to those ancient people which is still the most popular Bible verse to be incorporated into modern marriages. It says, 'Love is patient, love is kind. It does not envy, it does not boast, it is not proud. It does not dishonor others, it is not self-seeking, it is not easily angered, it keeps no record of wrongs. Love does not delight in evil but rejoices with the truth. It always protects, always trusts, always hopes, always perseveres.' You see, my friends, God has given us through these words, a checklist of recognizing what true love is. He teaches us, through this passage, how to love each other. How to form a successful partnership with the person you love. If we follow this teaching, not only our marriages, but all our human interactions will be blessed by God. Paul continues, 'And now these three remain: faith, hope and love. But the greatest of these is love.'"

Pastor Ralph closed his Bible and laid it on a small wooden perch. "I've been lucky enough to know Shaw for a long, long time. He's been a faithful member of the congregation of Oceanview Church for several decades. His daughter, Sadie has also made Oceanview her church home and I know what a faithful and loving family the two of them have. Recently I was honored to meet Nora as well. You may be wondering why this graceful beast has a place of honor at this wedding." He gestured to Thunder and laughter rippled through the attendees. "Thunder used to belong to Nora's Aunt Edie who once owned this beautiful property. When Edith moved into a medical facility for her final days, she sold Thunder to a new owner. When Nora moved in, Thunder was one of her first visitors. The horse had an uncanny sense that someone related to his beloved Edith had moved into the mansion, and he escaped his new owners' property and mysteriously showed up here. He didn't just escape once, he made his intentions clear by doing it numerous times. Nora called in the vet who cared for Thunder, and behold, it was Shaw."

The audience chuckled again.

"Not only was Thunder the matchmaker who brought these two together, but he's now at the center of a venture the two of them have partnered in, providing equine therapy to the sick and disabled. So, you see, friends, it is right and good that Thunder takes a prominent place in this wedding."

The pastor moved on to the vows and the rings, and before Sadie knew it, Nora and her dad were facing their guests, hands held high, being introduced for the first time as Mr. and Mrs. Shaw and Nora Flynn. Tears of happiness appeared on her cheeks and she wiped them away. Her father so deserved this moment, this present, this future of happiness. And so did Nora.

The happy couple stepped down from the pagoda, basking in the joy from their friends. As they passed Sadie, her dad lifted his hand and she gave it a high five. They headed for the mansion, and the guests filtered out, row by row to join them.

Sadie glanced up. Heart pounding, she saw that Jett had lingered. Soon, it was just the two of them in the pasture, surrounded by empty white folding chairs. He kept his distance. He'd made the first step by showing up. The next step was up to her.

"Hi," she called quietly.

His handsome face beamed with a grin at her single word. "Hey, Sadie." He made his way over to her. He gazed into her eyes and she waited quietly, soaking in the cocoa brown of his irises.

"I came because I really needed to talk to you. And you were ignoring my calls."

"I know. I'm sorry. That was a really immature way of dealing with this. I'm not proud of myself whatsoever."

He shrugged. "It's okay. You're not supposed to be perfect. I mean, it gives the rest of us hope."

She looked confused. "What do you mean?"

"I mean, you're invincible. You can do anything. You set the bar so high. Look at what you've accomplished just over the last few weeks. You learned to sail. You competed in a prestigious race and placed fourth. I'm guessing you passed your nursing test. And you planned this stunning wedding and day of love for your dad and his bride. I mean, seriously. Is there anything you can't do?"

His smile lightened her heart. But he was sugar-coating it. And she had to call him on it. "I didn't learn how to recognize a coral reef in the dark."

"I know. But I can't think of any novice sailors who could. Can you please just put that one incident out of your mind, and accept the fact that you're amazing?"

She shook her head. She attempted to speak, only to realize that she didn't know where to start. She looked at him, and her heart turned sad. Because she knew she had to be honest with him. And when she was done, he would walk away from her, forever.

She gestured to the chairs. "Can we sit?" They did, and he took her hands in his. She would've disallowed it, except that her hands were shaking, and she needed his strength. "I shared with you the story of my parents' marriage."

"Yes, on the boat. They rushed into marriage, didn't know each other well, and it turned out to be a disaster."

"On the surface, yes, all those things are true. But that could actually describe almost half the marriages out there. Sad, but true. No. My whole childhood was a living example of how making the wrong decision about the one you love can cause pain and chaos for everyone involved."

Jett squeezed her hands. "I can understand that. I'm sorry for what you went through and I know this day was a long time in coming, but look what happened today. Your father got his happy ending."

"Yes, and I'm so happy for him, for them. But I'm talking about us, too, Jett. I mean, I'm trying to."

"Good, because that's why I'm here. That's why I crashed your dad's wedding, Sadie. I could see no other way to get to talk to you about what happened. You and I did the race, and then you just disappeared completely out of my life. If you don't want to see me anymore, I'll have to accept that. But please, just tell my why. I'll be tortured for the rest of my life if I don't know why."

Tears welled in her eyes and he released her hand to brush them gently off her cheeks.

"I'm sorry. I don't have any experience with relationships. But I've told myself my entire life that I won't allow what happened to my parents to happen to me. It's why I've been so cautious about dating. I don't want to find myself in a bad relationship like my parents'."

"What is scaring you about being with me?" he asked quietly.

She blinked. "I really like you, Jett. We have a lot of interests in common, and I love your ambition in the world of sailing. You taught me an extreme sport that I think I could be crazy about, yacht sailing. But when I look at the foundation of our relationship, I just don't think we can get past it."

Jett was listening. She'd grabbed his attention. He was speechless as he stared at her.

"By running The Majestic over the reef, I singlehandedly did three things to you. Detrimental things. Three ways I hurt you. I damaged the boat that you love. I made you lose to the father who has abused you for years. And I lost you the contract for the invention that you've been working so hard on. With my one careless, no, *clueless*, action, I did all that damage. And yes, I know," she said, interrupting his protests, "you've said you can forgive me for all that. But I don't believe you're thinking straight. How can you possibly put all that behind you? If we started a relationship, it would be on a rocky foundation. It would be doomed from the start, just like my parents'. It may not be immediately, but my mistake would someday raise its ugly head and be a source of contention between us. Everyone thinks their love is strong when they first commit to each other. Even my father thought that my mother was the love of his life. Until they started living life together. And that's when it starts to disintegrate."

She sniffed. "So, I'm sorry, Jett. I need to end this love between us before it really even begins." She dropped his hand and stood. "I need to get to the reception, ..."

"Wait." He stood too. "Let me just ask you this. Do you love me, Sadie?"

She stared into his earnest face. He wanted an answer, but she had no idea what to say. She'd never been in love. What did she have to compare it to?

Then her mind ran to Pastor Ralph's words today. *Love is patient, love is kind.* She looked at Jett with new eyes, her mind whirring. Jett patiently taught her to sail, even though he only had a couple of weeks to complete the job before the race. He never yelled at her, never became frustrated with her lack of knowledge. He was always kind, without fail.

Love always protects, always trusts. As her eyes flicked between both of his, her brain flooded with all the ways Jett had protected her on the race. He'd saved her from a shark attack, putting himself in physical harm. By allowing them both a sleeping shift, Jett sacrificed a potential win in the race but did it because he was protecting her from future mistakes she'd make sailing the ship alone.

He always trusted her, even when she didn't deserve it. He treated her like a true partner, despite her inexperience in sailing. Would he also treat her like that in love?

Love always hopes, always perseveres. Unlike herself, Jett hadn't given up hope on a relationship between the two of them. Despite her blatant avoidance, he persevered, even going so far as crashing her father's wedding so he could see her.

Jett demonstrated what true love was. He showed her what true love looked like.

Jett's love was true. He'd told her, and now he'd shown her, and even the Bible proved it. But what about her? Did she love him too? Setting aside her fear that her mistake had provided a rocky foundation for a relationship, *did she love him*?

Judging by her misery and sadness over the last few weeks since her return from Bermuda, she would say, yes. This must be what love felt like.

Grabbing her courage and her strength, she said, "Yes, Jett. I love you."

Chapter Eighteen

Jett's heart shifted into overdrive and he grabbed her around the waist, lifted her off her feet, swinging her around with happiness. She loved him. She'd just said so.

"Wait, wait, wait," she protested.

He set her down and held onto her arms until she could stand on her own.

"I do love you, Jett, but it doesn't change anything. It doesn't change everything I've explained about a rocky foundation. Haven't you been listening to a word I've said?"

Jett couldn't help the glowing smile that covered his face. "Yes, Sadie, I've been listening. In fact, I've been waiting almost two weeks to be able to listen to you. I've been driving myself crazy wondering why you left me like that. I'm listening, believe me."

She pulled out of his arms. "In that case, I hope you agree with me. I didn't mean to be rude and break off ties completely. I hope that some-day we can be friends again. But I hope you realize that we can't be to-gether." She took a step backward. She studied his face and frowned. "Jett, why do you have that ridiculous smile?"

"Because! Sadie, listen to me now. When I got home from Bermu-da and you refused to speak to me, I was so distraught. I asked God for help. You taught me that God cares about the big things in our lives as well as the tiny little things. And this, this seemed like a huge thing. So, I prayed to God for guidance. And he gave it."

Sadie shook her head. "What do you mean?"

Jett held up one finger. "Your concerns, one by one. You damaged my boat. It's already fixed, Sadie. I hired a professional boat repair company and they worked on it right away. It's as good as new. I've sailed on it several times and it's watertight. Old boats need maintenance all the time. This is just one more thing. So that problem ... gone."

He held up a second finger. "My dad beat me in the race. Yeah, well, so what? He is the more talented racer. I have to give him credit where credit's due. Could we have beat him without the flooding? Maybe. But, it doesn't matter. It's one race, Sadie."

"But," she protested, "he was so mean to you. He humiliated you in Bermuda. I caused that."

He let out a dismissive snort. "One of many, sweetheart. I'm not going to let you take responsibility for our horrible relationship. It's been going on my entire life. You had nothing to do with that."

She let out a deep sigh.

"I will beat my father someday. And maybe that will be the catalyst for him developing some respect for me. But again, not your battle."

She shook her head. "Okay, so your boat is fixed, and your father is unfixable. But the biggest thing I lost you was the Sailtone contract. I could never forgive myself for that, and you shouldn't either."

He gazed at her beauty, his heart beating in his chest, a smile covering his face.

"What?" she asked suspiciously.

He shook his head. "I got the contract."

"What?"

"I'm waiting on the paperwork, but they're moving into manufacturing. Life's about to change, Sadie, and it was only because of you."

She shook her head. "No, me? I had nothing to do with your invention. That was all you."

He took her shoulders firmly with his hands and leaned close. "No. Think back. I'd injured myself and couldn't sail alone. I needed a partner. All my experienced sailing friends turned me down. There was only one person who believed in me, who was willing to put her own life aside, face the chance of failing her classes, flunking her test, because of the kind, generous person she was. My savior. That was you, Sadie."

She gasped.

"You are the reason I'm moving into manufacturing with my invention. That race gave me visibility. I placed fourth, but it didn't matter. The time was right. I'd say that makes us a pretty strong team. And gives our love a very strong foundation." He pulled her in for a kiss, and this time she didn't resist, she didn't argue. She kissed him back.

When they paused, she was gazing at him with wonder in her eyes. She whispered, "God took an impossible situation and made it good."

Jett nodded. "God cleared the way for us."

Their lips met again, and Jett's body filled with relief. She was in his arms where she belonged, and she'd said she loved him. Just to be sure, and just so he could hear it with his own two ears, he pulled back. "I love you, Sadie."

Her beautiful face beamed with an unfettered smile. "And I love you too, Jett. Now and forever."

Epilogue

Four months later

Jett climbed to the top of The Majestic's mast and examined the horizon. They were on the last stretch of the Carolina Pride yacht race. They'd started this morning at the north end of North Carolina, and they would finish in the next few minutes, God willing, in Hilton Head Island on the southern tip of South Carolina.

It had been a glorious day, and he wasn't just thinking of the bright sunshine. This race was monumental for several reasons.

His rib was healed, and his body had returned to full sailing ability.

He was sailing in his second-ever double-handed race. In fact, he may be placing single-handed racing in his rearview mirror for good. Double-handed racing was so much more fun, especially considering his first mate was the love of his life.

Once he and Sadie had mutually removed all the perceived barriers, their love and partnership had grown exponentially. He'd never been this happy in his life, and he knew without a doubt that Sadie felt the same way. Not only did she continue to tell him how happy she was, they had formed a relationship built on the strongest of foundations: honesty, love and faith.

He had continued to train Sadie on her sailing techniques, and this race marked their foray into a double-handed sailing partnership that few could beat. At least, that was their mutual goal.

Visualizing the placement of the rest of the competing yachts as they approached the finish line, Jett began his climb down the mast.

"Hey, wait, man. Hold on. That makes a great shot."

Jett swallowed a protest. Mason being on the yacht with them while they raced was another reason this race was different. Jett was now a professional sailor, sponsored by Sailtone. Therefore, he was forced to agree to certain things that were normally at odds to his mindset. Such as, posing for pictures during an important race that would eventually be used in commercials and promos for his sail sunscreen product, which would be hitting the open market in a few months' time.

"Yeah, stud, you look hot up there! Smile!" Sadie's voice rose to him from her place behind the helm. He grimaced at her. She knew how much he hated that part of his new success. But thank God, she helped him deal with it with a sense of humor.

"Grab a photo while you can because I've got a race to win," he shouted down to Mason, who was snapping away on his big camera.

He reached the cabin and joined Sadie behind the wheel. "I don't have time for this nonsense," he muttered.

"Oh, stop your grumbling. The whole world will fall in love with you once they see you in action captaining a boat."

He reached for the starboard line and tugged on it. "I only want one person to fall in love with me. You."

"Hey," she reminded him. "I'm already in love with you, Captain."

His heart skipped a beat and he leaned in for a kiss. Mason caught the kiss on film. Jett groaned and went back to work. "Ready to jibe?"

"Ready to jibe!" Sadie shouted and got into place.

They worked together, maneuvering the thirty-three-foot yacht. Jett yelled out orders to propel them to the finish line. Sadie understood his commands and executed on them smoothly. As they raced, Jett kept his eyes on their competitors while Sadie kept her eyes on the sails.

The finish line was in sight. Jett took the helm and steered The Majestic speedily over the virtual line well ahead of all other yachts. Once they had safely won the race, Sadie and Mason jumped up and down, cheering their win. Jett chuckled as he slowed the yacht, steered it towards its slip and lowered the sails.

Later, when the yacht was secured, they wandered over to the medals stand. Spectators lined the dock and several of them held hands out to Jett to shake with their congratulations. He slipped an arm around Sadie's shoulder. They were a team. It was her win, too.

Yachts continued to cross the finish line. Jett stared at the one approaching now. "Hey Sadie," he said, and pointed. "Take a look at that boat."

Sadie gasped. "Oh my gosh. Is that ...?"

"Yep," Jett responded, sure now. "The Wolverine. I wasn't even aware my dad was in this race." He watched as the boat crossed the line in what Jett guessed was sixth or seventh place. "I wonder if he had trouble out there."

They stood on the dock while all the boats finished, then the awards presentation ceremony was about to start. The crowd thickened, and Jett waited, a sense of anxiety forming in his throat. He wasn't anxious about taking the podium for his first-place win. He was anxious about facing his father. He glanced at Sadie and she seemed to read his mind. She pulled him closer and rested her head on his shoulder.

He didn't have to wait long. "Hey, son," came a voice behind him. They turned. His father looked tired. Exhausted might be a better word. His eyes drooped, and his stance was bent.

"Are you okay, Dad?"

His father searched Jett's face. "Yeah, I'm fine. That race beat me up."

"What happened?"

"Caught the edge of a plastic barrel bobbing in the ocean. Didn't see it till we were right up on it. Ran over it, but it got caught in the rudder. Had to stop and pull it out of the blades."

Jett grimaced. It had happened to him before. "Sometimes you get a bad break, and there's nothing you can do about it."

"Hello, Mr. Martin," said Sadie, holding out her hand.

Jett's dad focused on her. "Cameron," he corrected. "And you are ... remind me."

"Sadie Flynn. Jett's partner." Sadie gave his father a smile and pulled Jett closer to her side. The old man would have to be blind to miss the implication.

The sound of a shutter clicking caused Jett to turn to Mason, who was capturing the entire greeting on film. "Oh, and this is Mason, Dad. Mason is my rep from my new sponsor, Sailtone."

Jett would've laughed at the look of amazement on his dad's face, if he hadn't turned over a new leaf, with God's help. His entire childhood, Jett had wanted to show up his father, to beat him at his own game. To smear his father's face in his own success. Today, that time had come.

But God had shown him the right way to handle the situation, the gracious way, the Christian way. There would be no smearing or trash talking today.

"Mason, this is my father, Cameron Martin. He's a yacht captain too."

Mason held his hand out. "Of course, I've heard of you, Captain Martin. You must be so proud of your son. Winning this race, gaining a sponsor and patenting an invention that's going to market under Sailtone."

His dad stared, shook his head as if to clear out his ears, then stared some more. Jett took pity on him. It wasn't his dad's fault Jett had kept all these accomplishments a secret from him. Well, on second thought, it was partly his dad's fault.

"Dad, why don't you stick around after the medals ceremony? You, me and Sadie can sit down for a drink and get caught up. Would you like that?"

Dad's face cleared. He reached out a hand and gripped Jett's. "Yes, son, thank you. I would like that."

The air crackled with the magnified voice of the announcer. "And now, the results of the thirty fifth sailing of the Carolina Pride Yacht Race. Sailors, please make your way to the podium."

As the announcer began with the third-place finishers, Dad said softly, "Congratulations, son. I'm proud of all your accomplishments."

Jett turned and faced his dad. A stab hit his throat. He wanted to respond, to thank him, to recognize what a huge moment this was, but he couldn't speak. His dad gave him a nod, patted his shoulder, turned and walked into the crowd.

"And the first-place finishers of this year's Carolina Pride Yacht race, Jett Martin and Sadie Flynn! Jett and Sadie, come on up to the podium for your trophies."

Sadie started to pull him, but he had something to do first. The trophy could wait. This couldn't. He pulled her back to face him and capture her undivided attention. He rested his lips on hers for a slow, passionate kiss. Her beating heart rested against his chest.

"Hey Sadie," he said when they parted. "Will you marry me?"

Her eyes opened wide and her mouth followed. The crowd around them went silent. Nothing mattered except him and her, and her answer to his question.

"Jett! Are you crazy? We have a trophy to accept."

"I have to know. I'm not saying today. I'm not even saying tomorrow. But I know God placed us together as a team and it's not just to win races together. It's to be in love for the rest of our lives. I'm ready. Are you?"

Once the words were out of his mouth, he realized what an egregious error this would be if she said no.

But she didn't.

"Yes, Jett Martin! Yes, I will marry you!"

She not only said it, she shouted it so that all those around them could hear. A small scattering of applause surrounded them. He kissed her again, and then led her through the crowd in the direction of the podium.

They had a trophy to accept.

THE END

Leave a review!

Did you love Jett and Sadie's? If you did please go here[1], and leave a review! Reviews help so much to guide readers to find good books to read! Thank you for supporting *Capsized*, me, and Christian fiction!

Laurie's Letter to Readers

Hello everyone!

I want to take a moment to extend a really big THANK YOU for reading my book, *Capsized*. I presume that you have read more of my books than just this one, and that warrants another really big THANK YOU. I've created quite a library now of inspirational romance novels and I'm enjoying it so much. It's only because of you guys who love what I'm doing, and wait for each one, that I am able to live my dream.

I began writing *Capsized* in a hotel in Tennessee when my parents and I had evacuated our homes in Pawleys Island and Murrells Inlet, SC in the throes of Hurricane Florence. We were staying in beautiful Kodak, TN while our beach communities were getting pummeled with wind and rain. To fill the long days, I started writing. With the plotting help of some of my closest writer friends, I came up with this plot about Sadie, who you met in Book 1: *Sanctuary*, and her eventual hero, Jett. I made Sadie a daredevil, an extreme sport athlete, so of course, she needed someone with similar interests to give her a run for her money. I wanted an extreme sport that is beachy and settled on competitive yacht sailing.

Great! Except I've never sailed a sailboat. And I knew I would have to learn or else the story would fail. Errors in a fiction storyline pull an informed reader right out of the story. Some small "errors" are forgivable if they don't affect the plot or the storyline. But writing a book about sailing and making mistakes about sailing basics is definitely not acceptable.

So I reached out and connected with three fantastic sailing experts. All three of these generous sailors were "volunteered" by people I know to help me with their sailing expertise. When I reached out to them for help I had already written about twenty pages with sailing content. I explained what I wanted from them – to correct all my technical errors. They read the sailing pages and wrote back with corrections, suggestions, ideas. Consolidating all their feedback, I went back through the pages and made updates and sent them out again. I still hadn't gotten it completely right, so they sent me back feedback again. Now, I feel confident that the sailing content is "right enough" not to be disruptive to the storyline. If there are still errors that remain, first of all, they're entirely mine. And second, they don't hurt the story.

So, my great thanks to my three sailors: **Charity Monroe, Tim McKenney** and **Paul McNamee**. I truly could NOT have written this book without you!

Another expert I need to mention is **Tricia Martin**. Tricia was my inspiration for Sadie's character from Day One when I decided she would be a dedicated extreme athlete. I used to work with Tricia in my previous career, and one Monday she walked into work, full of her normal energy, and revealed to me that she'd just ran a marathon the day before. Instead of limping down the hall, or better yet, taking the day off to recover, she breezed in just like it was any other day. After expressing my shock at her physical fitness, she shared that she had made a goal to run a marathon in all fifty states. AND she was well on her way to completing it.

I called Tricia after I'd created Sadie. We talked about what is inside a marathoner's brain and spirit to make her keep running, keep training, through the pain and the discomfort. I hope I did justice to Sadie's marathon scene. A lot of it incorporated Tricia's input.

So, sometimes it takes a "village" to write a novel and I'd like to thank the knowledgeable peeps from my village of dedicated athletes who helped me get this one right. Enjoy "your" book. And readers, hope you enjoy it too.

Love,

Laurie

About Laurie

Laurie just completed a 34-year career with a major Fortune 50 company. She's very proud of all that she accomplished there. For 19 of those years, she also wrote books and published 20 novels. Now, she finds herself in her dream-come-true position. She retired from the big day job, sold her house in the Midwest, lives three miles from the beach in her beloved South Carolina and writes whenever she wants.

Laurie will be celebrating her 30th wedding anniversary this year, as well the marriage of one of her two sons. She plans one more book in the Murrells Inlet Miracles series before launching a new series about matchmakers.

Want to stay in touch with Laurie?

Her website/blog[1]
Her Facebook[2]
Her Twitter[3]
Her Bookbub[4]
Her Goodreads[5]

Sign up to be on her <u>newsletter mailing list</u>[6]! You'll get advance notice of all reviews, chances to win prizes and receive free books and other giveaways!

Other Christian Fiction novels

by Laurie Larsen
The Murrells Inlet Miracles series:

---

1. http://authorlaurielarsen.com/

2. https://www.facebook.com/authorlaurielarsen

3. https://twitter.com/AuthorLaurie

4. https://www.bookbub.com/authors/laurie-larsen

5. https://www.goodreads.com/author/show/412692.Laurie_Larsen

6. https://www.authorlaurielarsen.com/reader-group

Book 1: Sanctuary[7]: Successful Philadelphia attorney Nora Ramsey never even knew there was another life for her before Aunt Edie left her with her ramshackle mansion and once-thriving horse business. Veterinarian Shaw Flynn seems a partner, then a love interest, before finding out his deepest and darkest secret.

Book 2: Restoration[8]: Young, single mom Carly Milner was making it on her own raising her toddler Grace and finishing her education so she could launch her professional career. When the love of her life, Ryan Melrose returns, wanting a place in Grace's life, can she ever trust him again?

---

7. https://www.authorlaurielarsen.com/sanctuary

8. https://www.authorlaurielarsen.com/restoration

Book 3: Crescendo:[9] A rags to riches story in the world of country music, with a twist! Black sheep in a wealthy family Haley Witherspoon has finally found the career that brings her passion, and it's with handsome aspiring country musician, Blake Scott. Can they overcome her family's disapproval, his own internal guilt, mounting danger from a fan to achieve success?

Book 4: Capsized:[10] God "overseas" everything. Two highly competitive extreme athletes pair up to achieve victory in the world of competitive yacht sailing. With physical attraction tempting them, Sadie and

---

9. https://www.authorlaurielarsen.com/crescendo

10. https://www.authorlaurielarsen.com/capsized

Jett must keep their eyes on the prize. But God has other plans. As they face adversity and danger, will God's will have them racing toward one another instead of the glory of the win?

The Pawleys Island Paradise series:

Book 1: <u>Roadtrip</u> <u>to Redemption</u>[1]. *It started as a trip to lose old memories. It became a journey to find her heart.* A woman facing the most desolate summer of her life, follows God's direction and instead has the most rewarding and life-changing summer of all.

Book 2: Tide to Atonement[2]. *Life knocked him down. Faith raised him up.* A man has paid his debt to society and is released from prison. Determined to create a life to be proud of, he realizes his past isn't quite as willing to be done as he wants it to be.

---

1. https://www.authorlaurielarsen.com/roadtrip-to-redemption

2. https://www.authorlaurielarsen.com/tide-to-atonement

Book 3: Journey to Fulfillment[3]. *A traumatic family event. Distinctly opposite ways of dealing with it between husband and wife. Let no man put asunder.* A married couple deals with a family tragedy in different ways and works through the resulting collapse of their marriage to reconcile their love for each other.

Book 4: Bridge to Fruition[4]. *The old is gone. The new is come.* A young woman from an affluent family finds love with a man who grew up in the foster system. Can they let go of the trappings of their past and find love together in their present?

---

3. https://www.authorlaurielarsen.com/journey-to-fulfillment

4. https://www.authorlaurielarsen.com/bridge-to-fruition

Book 5: Path to Discovery[5]. A brokenhearted New York actress welcomes the escape from the hustle and bustle of the big city to take the lead in a beach-town dinner theater show. It's the solace and sanctuary that she's needed ever since her world came crumbling down. But then he walks in... back into her life and her memories of her worst nightmare.

Book 6: Return to Devotion[6]. *Can men and women be "just friends?"* A military wife deals with unbearable loneliness on her husband's third overseas deployment, leading to an indiscretion with her new male friend. Will the truth destroy everything she and her husband have built as man and wife?

---

5. https://www.authorlaurielarsen.com/path-to-discovery

6. https://www.authorlaurielarsen.com/path-to-discovery

Book 7: <u>Pawleys</u> <u>Island Paradise:</u> <u>A Companion</u>[7]. Discover the stories and inspiration that led to the Pawleys Island Paradise series! A short, fully-illustrated non-fiction companion to the beloved Pawleys Island Paradise series of inspirational romance by award-winning author Laurie Larsen.

<u>Pawleys</u> <u>Island Paradise boxset</u>[8]: First three books in one easy download!

Preacher Man[9]. Laurie's 2010 EPIC Award winner for Best Spiritual Romance of 2010: A beautiful, heartwarming Christian love story that will leave you feeling good.

9. https://www.authorlaurielarsen.com/preacher-man

Don't miss out!

Visit the website below and you can sign up to receive emails whenever Laurie Larsen publishes a new book. There's no charge and no obligation.

https://books2read.com/r/B-A-WTLE-ILGW

BOOKS 2 READ

Connecting independent readers to independent writers.

www.ingramcontent.com/pod-product-compliance
Lightning Source LLC
Chambersburg PA
CBHW030329180626
46810CB00003B/1287